Th

The Duke of Darkness

OLIVER WOOD

Table of Contents

THE BEGINNING

Wherever in the world, when the darkness of night approaches, the seven canisters begin to glow.

All seven are scattered across the Earth's continents, buried deep in the darkest of places. Waiting to be found.

These canisters do not belong in our world; it is important you understand this. How they arrived on Earth is a mystery that even the greatest of minds cannot solve.

Somebody, though, somewhere, somehow, has the knowledge of their arrival, and in the end, the truth will become known. But for now, their secrets are buried with each of them, and only the rumours reach the surface.

Dangerous rumours.

Legend has it that these tubular canisters are made from glass stronger than steel. Metallic glass.

But it is the liquid that lies inside that matters the most. A syrupy, almost fluorescent liquid as poisonous to the world as it is magnificent.

Once found, the neon glow of the liquid, and the pull of human curiosity, will force the finder and keeper to take a drink.

That first taste will provide the new owner with powers that are beyond anyone's imagination.

Like a hungry infection, each potion snakes its way into the bloodstream. Exploring every cell of the body, invading the thought processes of the mind, and seeking the soul of its new master. It twists and turns and wriggles and winds…

Providing the power that every human craves.

The legends say that no canister is the same. Each one offers their own set of powers that will transform its chosen one. And they will be chosen.

Seven canisters. Seven different colours. Seven different powers.

Whisperings of these powers have spread.

Warnings…

The owner will be given the strength of a thousand men and blessed with a supreme, razor-sharp mind.

But the powers run deeper…

The potion will supply its finder and keeper with an ambition that is more powerful than strength and intellect. Its owner will be filled with a desire to conquer and rule. To take over the world and destroy everything that stands in its way.

And deeper still...

The keeper of the canister will be gifted with a special power to match their ambition. This power, unique to the liquid they drink, is the deadliest of them all.

A power like no other...

A power that is way beyond what humans are capable of...

A power that creates a new species at the top of the food chain...

A power that could destroy the world as we know it.

Congratulations. You are one of the first to know. Our only hope is for the seven canisters to remain hidden.

Chapter 1

30 DAYS UNTIL MISSION

Alfie Andrews was being watched.

It wasn't by people who would usually watch a ten-year-old boy at his local school. Not by a dinner lady in the playground for kicking a puddle in an attempt to soak their friends and anybody else unlucky enough to be within splashing distance. Not by their teacher in a lesson for sneaking a glance at Daisy Donnelley's test paper because she hadn't got a question wrong for over three years. Not even by the head teacher, for drifting off into a 'boredom-free' sleep during yet another painfully dull morning assembly.

Alfie Andrews was being watched by two men; men who didn't belong in his safe and perfectly normal world.

It had been happening for a few weeks. The first time he spotted these two unusual characters was at lunch time in the dinner hall. Noise had circulated the room as Alfie opened his lunchbox to reveal the contents of the day's meal: a banana that looked like it had been involved in a cage fight – and lost, and one of his mother's 'experimental' sandwiches. In other words, 'open the fridge and chuck in the first thing she could see' sandwich. The result was a combination of chopped onion and mustard. Alfie slammed his lunchbox shut before the foul aroma could invade the entire room. Blushing, his large eyes, one blue and one green, covered slightly by strands of his blonde wispy hair, darted around the space. He feared hundreds of pairs of eyes would be glaring at him. But there were only two. The two men.

And then they were gone.

The second time was later that week during another painfully dull maths lesson taught by the even more painfully dull Mrs Fullylove, along with her high-pitched voice.

"If you take a look at this fraction, you will soon realise that it needs to be simplified, children!" she screeched, with a tone similar to a cat who had just unfortunately had its tail trodden on. "Pay close attention to the numerator and denominator and follow the process which I will go over AGAIN…"

Eardrums were bursting around the local area and all dogs were heading in the direction of the school. To block out the deafening tone, Alfie had spent the entire lesson attempting to guess the age of the wrinkled, spectacle-wearing teacher by observing her closely. The constant chatter of the class as she attempted to teach the method of simplifying fractions indicated that her hearing was in desperate need of repair; her lipstick-stained teeth suggested her eyesight was becoming rather blurry despite the oversized, thick-framed glasses that scarily magnified her eyes; and Alfie was sure that she had shrunk at least two inches in the two terms he had been imprisoned in her class. As Mrs Fullylove limped over to her chair and slumped into it, relief spreading across her face, Alfie decided that her age had to be at least 102. Happy with his new estimate, Alfie gazed idly out of the window. Again, the same two men filled the space.

And then they were gone.

The third and most recent sighting was in the playground. Alfie was stood watching a group of children loyally following one particular boy around like a dog obeying its master. The boy was Connor Deangelo. Connor was like an unstoppable robot created by the world's greatest scientist: he had the build of a boxer, the brains of a champion chess player, and the sporting ability of every Olympic gold medallist, in every Olympic sport, in the history of the Olympics all rolled into one. To the other boys in the school, he was a Ferrari in a scrapyard; to the girls, he was Prince Charming. But Connor Deangelo had one malfunction: he was a horrible human being. (HHB). And Alfie, now joined by his best friend Faz, was witnessing this malfunction in action.

HHB Example 1: Connor began telling anyone who would listen (which was everyone) that, perhaps, his most faithful dog, Michael Madison, was wearing a pair of his sister's red, frilly knickers. News travelled across the playground and a Mexican wave of laughter erupted, forcing the poor boy to turn the colour of his sister's underwear and run off in tears.

One dog down.

"Now he'll target a group of them," said Faz, flicking a gold coin into the air and catching it in his hand. "It's to prove he can dominate groups of children as well as individuals…"

HHB Example 2: Connor had lined up all of his adoring fans in the order of who he liked the least. The bottom three were judged to be too ugly (she had three rather long hairs sticking out of her oversized mole), too boring (he kept on talking about pencil museums) or too fat (he had about nine chins). Connor's decisions resulted in the bottom three running off in tears.

Four dogs down.

"He's proved his verbal dominance," continued Faz, as if narrating a wildlife programme. "His insults have been his chosen weapon. Now for the physical attack…"

HHB Example 3: Rope of Death. Connor was now wildly skimming a heavy rope along the floor in a circular motion, causing the rest of his dog litter to jump in an attempt to avoid their legs being chopped off. Each rotation saw the deadly rope increase in height. Remaining members of the 'King Connor Clan', too loyal or stupid to run, began jumping like frantic frogs. Ruby Samuels mistimed her jump, somersaulted in the air and landed on her head, and the featherweight Freddie Draper somehow managed to become tangled in the rope and was swept along for the ride.

All dogs down.

Faz offered a few final thoughts, but his words

were lost on Alfie. The two men were now stood in his playground.

And this time, they remained.

They towered above everything else like buildings dominating the skyline. Both were immaculately dressed in matching dark suits and wore dominant sunglasses that glistened in the morning sunshine, similar to the shoes on their feet. One was straightening his already perfect tie as the other held a clipboard that was swallowed up in his huge hands. Every other child in the playground seemed blissfully unaware of their presence.

Alfie had no idea how long he had been staring but was suddenly interrupted by the ear-splitting sound of the bell. Before he knew it, once again, they had gone.

The only difference this time is that they clearly wanted to be seen.

Chapter 2

28 DAYS UNTIL MISSION

There were many things that Alfie Andrews hated about school. Right at the top of his list was parents' evening. Alfie had remembered last year's meeting when Pleasant Grove Academy had decided to force the children to attend with their parents. Fifteen of the slowest and most painful minutes saw his parents and his teacher, Mrs Mulberry, enjoy the welcome opportunity to take Alfie's personality and chop it up into tiny little pieces, as if it was an onion from his lunchbox. The first half of the session followed the route of discussing Alfie as though he was completely invisible, before finally acknowledging his presence through a series of questions:

Alfie, why do you only complete half a page of writing in an hour? (Alfie's Father).

Alfie, why are you doodling 'YNTR' instead of

exploring the wonderful world of fractions? (Mrs Mulberry—asked on behalf of Mrs Fulllylove, using her words). (YNTR stood for You Need To Retire).

Alfie, why are you saying that the dog ate your homework when you know the only pet, we have is a goldfish? (Alfie's Mother).

The meeting ended with Mrs Mulberry clearly stating the targets for Alfie's improvement.

Become more involved in class discussion. Complete a greater amount of work in the time available. Be more consistent with homework. Realise that these are the most important years of your life. Be more proactive during group tasks. Show willingness to take your learning beyond the classroom. Stop making goldfish impressions during creative writing…

This year, however, was different. His teacher was Mr Spencer. Mr Spencer had only been at the school for a few months, but already had become the most popular teacher in the school. The girls were captivated by his welcoming smile and sharp dress sense, and the boys admired his slick football skills during his enjoyable PE lessons. His legendary status was confirmed when he demonstrated the 'flip-flap' skill made famous by a Brazilian footballer. The ball seemed to stick to his foot as he glided past the helpless defender. To the delight of everyone, the defender happened to be Connor Deangelo.

Mr Spencer was like no other teacher you would ever meet; he had the ability to make you feel that you were the most important child in the class.

Alfie sat outside his classroom, sandwiched between his parents. His father was aggressively tapping away on his work phone, probably sending yet another email to the army of people he was in charge of as a high-powered bank manager, while his mother was expertly applying another layer of brightly-coloured lipstick for the fifth time in as many minutes. They had the last appointment of the evening.

The door opened, and they were greeted by a smartly dressed Mr Spencer, wearing a dark blue shirt and bright yellow tie. His immaculate clothes were only outshone by his gleaming smile. "Alfie, great to see you! Mr and Mrs Andrews, please come in."

The classroom had been cleared of desks and four identical chairs remained, allowing everyone to take a seat. Mr Andrews was the last to sit down, busily sending a final email to another of his victims.

Mr Spencer waited patiently, ignoring the admiring stares from Alfie's mother.

"I would like to start by telling you how—"

"Well!" interrupted Mrs Andrews, "Alfie's certainly never had a teacher like you before. You look so young, so smart, so...dashing!"

Alfie sank into his chair.

"I have only recently started my teaching career," said Mr Spencer, coping extremely well with the uncomfortable atmosphere that Mrs Andrews had created. "And I must say, in the short period of time that I have taught your son, I can onl—"

"You're going to say exactly the same as every other teacher…" This time it was the turn of Mr Andrews to rudely interrupt, even though his eyes remained glued to his mobile phone. "…Alfie doesn't complete enough work in lessons, Alfie is always daydreaming instead of listening to the teacher, Alfie doesn't hand in his homework, Alfie would rather talk to his very few friends about football, even though we all know he's USELESS at it!" This time he did look up from his phone, only to stare into the eyes of Alfie as if he was one of his employees who had just cost the bank millions of pounds.

Silence filled the room and Alfie, to avoid any further evil stares, buried his chin deep into his chest, desperately hoping the ground would swallow him up.

The silence was eventually broken by Mrs Andrews who was still staring intently at Mr Spencer, whilst attempting to curl a lock of her hair around her index finger. "Well, it certainly sounds like you've been working very hard with the children, Mr Spencer. I'm sure Mrs Spencer misses you very much with all these long hours. Is there...a Mrs Spencer?"

"Your son has many talents that other teachers - and clearly yourselves - are unaware of," said Mr Spencer, ignoring the question.

This time the silence in the room was shared with a look of disbelief on the faces of the Andrews' family—including Alfie. Mr Spencer sat back in his chair, allowing the information to be absorbed and continued…

"I agree that Alfie could complete more work in lessons, but what he does produce is superb. In a recent English lesson, for example, his description of a chosen character for a story was, in my professional opinion, an exceptional piece of writing."

Alfie remembered the piece of writing well. What he liked most about Mr Spencer's lessons was that he allowed the class to make their own choices about their work. In this particular piece of writing, Alfie had decided to describe the two mysterious men.

"I'm sure you are keen to see this piece of work, Mr and Mrs Andrews," said Mr Spencer. "Alfie, after this meeting, please take your parents to the 'Wonderful Work' display board where you will find the piece of writing—I simply couldn't resist putting it up earlier today."

Alfie was suddenly filled with pride. It was a huge achievement to have a piece of work displayed on this board that took centre stage within the main corridor. It was usually reserved only for the most talented of children; for the likes of Connor Deangelo who was always keen to share the news with anyone who would listen.

"Yes—well we don't have time to start a tour of the school," replied Mr Andrews, now shifting in his seat in an attempt to end the meeting. "I've got to get back to the office, as my staff need my assistance."

"I'm sure your role at the bank is significant,

Mr Andrews," said Mr Spencer, "but your role as a parent is even more important."

Alfie could visibly see his father's throbbing forehead as he sat bolt upright in his chair. This meeting was far from over.

"Your son may not be the most gifted footballer in this school, but he is far from 'useless', Mr Andrews. An impressive quality that I have observed is his ability to run. What Alfie needs to realise is that there are many other sports to explore. I am currently in the process of organising a local schools' event that would suit your son's abilities." Mr Spencer gave Alfie a sudden wink that went unnoticed by his parents. Mr Andrews was too busy questioning his parenting skills, while Mrs Andrews was desperately trying to remove her wedding ring.

"Well, this all sounds wonderful about our little Alfie," said Mrs Andrews. "I always said to my husband that he was a talented boy. Now, if you have any concerns about him - and I mean any - then please do not hesitate to call me personally on my mobile number!" Mrs Andrews was now attempting to show Mr Spencer her ring-free left hand.

"Far more important than his qualities I have

already mentioned," continued Mr Spencer, "is the qualities of his character." Again, the three family members sat with the same confused look on their faces. "Allow me to explain. I believe—and have always believed—that in order to be the best version of yourself and be successful, you must have certain...attributes. Let's call them ingredients. I believe there are five ingredients that people require -"

"I believe that you are talking a load of nonsense!" interrupted Mr Andrews, pointing his chubby finger at Mr Spencer. "What you need in life is hard work!"

"Oh, I agree entirely," said Mr Spencer, skilfully both acknowledging and ignoring his point. "These five ingredients can be learnt and developed over a period of time—sometimes years. But certain people, and this is extremely rare...are born with them. These are the people who stand out above the rest..."

"What is your point, Mr Spencer?" said Mr Andrews impatiently.

"MACER!"

"Macer?" said both Mr and Mrs Andrews together.

"Modesty. Athleticism. Courage. Empathy.

Resilience. Place all of these ingredients together...and you have the perfect recipe."

Mr Andrews stood up in a fit of rage. His flushed cheeks began to slosh around as he shook his head furiously. "This is the biggest load of garbage I have ever heard. What rubbish do they teach you at these blinkin' teacher training places nowadays? When I was at school, you were told to work hard, or you'd get a clip round the ear. That's what my son needs to do...and if he doesn't, he'll see the back of my hand. Come on Maureen, we're off!"

Arthur Andrews pirouetted impressively for a large man and headed for the door, followed by his wife, who was still glancing admiringly at Mr Spencer.

"Mr Andrews!" Mr Spencer's voice was now much deeper and louder, causing the three family members to freeze as if they were playing a game of musical statues. "I also believe…" Mr Spencer moved towards the exit and opened the door before facing Alfie's father, "...that your son was born with all five of these attributes. He has the potential to do great things."

Chapter 3

Mr Spencer's words echoed in Alfie's mind as he led his parents in the direction of the 'Wonderful Work' display, much to the annoyance of Mr Andrews, who was still complaining about his teacher. "I mean who does he think he is talking to well-respected people like that? In my day, we looked up to our elders, especially a man in my position…"

His father's words faded into the distance. Instead, a never-ending list of questions were forming in Alfie's head: What did Mr Spencer see in him that others hadn't? What was this MACER code he lived by? What did resilient even mean? Was this the kind of report he had given to every child in the class? He would speak to Faz about it in the morning; maybe even find out what report Connor had received, even if it meant having a conversation with him and listening to how wonderful and talented, he thought he was.

Despite his mind feeling as though it had a

hive of bees buzzing around in it, Alfie felt fantastic. Better than he had felt in a very long time.

The corridors were now deserted and the late evening sun hibernated behind an angry cloud, darkening the surroundings. Alfie expected to be the only person, other than his parents, to be viewing the 'Wonderful Work' display at this time in the evening. He was wrong. Stood at the far end of the corridor were the now familiar figures of the two men, staring at the colourful image and scribbling down notes on the clipboard. This, Alfie realised, was the first time he had spotted them first.

He took advantage of this opportunity to study them further. The men, dressed identically in the same immaculate dark blue suits, looked even bigger than before. More powerful. The man closest had a shaven head and a strong jawline. His tanned, weathered skin clung to his skeletal face. He had the kind of face that had seen and been involved in many dark and dangerous things. A single teardrop tattoo was inked into his skin just below his right eye, a story of his past perhaps. Slowly, almost robotically, he turned his head to face Alfie, his slit-like eyes locking once again on his target. There was no reaction on his face, just an endless stare looking directly into Alfie's mind, reaching right into his soul.

The second man, clutching the ever present clipboard, made no attempt to acknowledge Alfie's presence. Instead, he continued to study the display, making notes without taking his eyes off the board in a manner almost as robotic as his partner. This man was without a doubt the largest man Alfie had ever seen. His neck, like a tree trunk, was heavily tattooed with images that would keep young children awake at night. But above all, it was the look in his steely eyes that really scared Alfie; a look that told him that whatever mission he had been given, he was programmed to carry it out right until the very end. And what worried Alfie even more, especially after realising it was his work that the giant was studying, was that it seemed like he was the mission.

The second man glanced towards his partner and nodded his head, indicating he had seen enough. The man closest broke free from his fixed stare and Alfie drew a breath for the first time in what seemed like a very long time. He watched as the two men turned their backs and slowly walked away. Only the footsteps of their polished shoes could be heard.

Alfie had forgotten that his parents were behind him. He wanted to see the look on their faces after seeing these two unforgettable individuals, but he was met by the familiar sight of his father buried in his mobile phone and his mother staring at her reflection in the window.

"Did you just see—"

"I've got to get back to the blinkin' office." Alfie was cut off by his father before he could finish the question. "These idiots—who I pay good money to—couldn't organise a smile at the circus! I feel like I'm running a blinkin' babysitting service rather than managing a bank. Come on Maureen, this display thingy will have to wait until next time. Alfie, let's go!"

Alfie watched as his father marched off in the opposite direction from the two men, closely followed by his wife. He moved into the position vacated by the giants and gazed at the display board. His work hung proudly in the centre. Alfie read the words out loud, attempting to guess the reasons why the two men had been studying it so closely; why they had been studying him so closely. Confused, Alfie shook the thoughts from his mind and turned to follow his parents. A yellow piece of paper lay on the floor in his path. Across the top, in bold blue writing, was the title: Operation Andrews. Alfie's chest pounded like a thousand drums. The rest of the page was filled with tiny writing that his eyesight couldn't quite make out. He slowly bent down to pick up the piece of paper, but stopped suddenly to check if he was being watched. Empty in both directions. He reached down, pinching the paper into his fingers clumsily, trying to stop his hands from shaking, too scared to look at the words but desperate for the information. This would be the answer to all of his questions over the past few weeks. His eyes rested on the sheet…

"ALFIE!" roared his father, now appearing at the far end of the corridor. "I. Need. To. Leave!"

Frustration flooded his entire body as Alfie realised that his father would wait no longer. He folded the piece of paper twice and carefully placed it in the front section of his bag, as if it was a map to find buried treasure, before sprinting in the direction of the now furious Mr Andrews.

Whatever was written on that piece of paper would have to wait until later.

Chapter 4

27 DAYS UNTIL MISSION

It was the day after the meeting with Mr Spencer and the previous evening had not gone to plan. Alfie had intended to go straight to bed in order to study the information on the piece of paper—to finally find out the reason why these two men had entered his life. His mother, however, had completely different ideas. With Mr Andrews back at the office, Mrs Andrews had decided to interrogate her son on the subject of her new project: Mr Spencer.

Actual Question: On which days are your PE sessions?

Hidden Meaning: Which days will she be able to see Mr Spencer wearing shorts?

Actual Question: Has Mr Spencer ever talked about family members?

Hidden Meaning: Does he have a wife? A

girlfriend? Any children? Is he at all available and, for some miracle, enjoys the company of overbearing housewives who wear far too much make-up?

Actual Question: How does he travel to and from school?

Hidden Meaning: Where does he live and how far will she have to travel when she begins stalking the poor man?

Actual Question: What does he like to eat?

Hidden Meaning: Does he have a sweet tooth so that she can bake her way into his heart through his stomach?

Actual Question: Does he have any hobbies or interests?

Hidden Meaning: Can she collect enough information about him in order to strike up a random conversation where she announces that she too enjoys hobbies such as windsurfing, kite boarding and skydiving at weekends?

Answering "I don't know, Mum," to every question frustrated Mrs Andrews, and the interrogation ended with her ordering Alfie to bed without any supper. To make matters worse, his bag remained in the kitchen so that Mrs Andrews could prepare one of her disastrous sandwiches for his lunch the following day. Alfie had spent the next two hours lying on his bed, desperately hoping for an opportunity to sneak back down to retrieve the information that was hidden in his school bag. Instead, his senses had taken an absolute battering: first, his nose had been invaded by a horrendous smell of cheese, meaning that his mother was creating the 'Triple B' sandwich for his lunch, consisting of mashed banana, beetroot and blue cheese. Following this, came the second wave of attack: this time on his ears as Mrs Andrews began her very own version of the song 'When A Man Loves A Woman,' clearly thinking about the possibility of Mr Spencer falling madly in love with her, which sounded similar to every car alarm in the street going off at once.

It had been a long and unsuccessful evening.

*

Alfie had arrived at school early with the hope of burying himself away in the corner of the playground so that he could read the piece of paper that was consuming his every thought. The early morning sun, bright and pleasant, was low in the sky and his chosen spot was shaded enough for Alfie to avoid squinting. Conditions were perfect.

Nervously excited, Alfie reached inside his school bag and carefully pulled out the treasure. He clutched the piece of paper in his hand as if it was a winning lottery ticket and unfolded it to reveal the title 'Operation Andrews'.

"What have you got there?"

The familiar, oversized shape of Faz appeared—standing with his hands on his hips—clearly trying to work out the reason why Alfie had taken up this unusual position in the school playground. Without waiting for an invitation, Faz clumsily collapsed down next to him.

"I've been looking everywhere for you…"

"Faz, I need to ask you something…" said Alfie gingerly, quickly stuffing the sheet of paper back into his bag. Faz had forgotten his original question and was now sat rotating his gold coin between his fingers. "Have you seen anyone…unusual in school lately…?"

"You mean Mrs Lafferty. I'm sure her woman beard is growing. First it just had a few whiskers, but now it's a full on man beard. Jimmy reckons she's got a special comb and beard gel for it, and the other day she was styling it in front of the little kids—they were all crying and running away according to Jimmy. She looks like she could play rugby for England—the ones that bury their faces in the other players' armpits—I bet she'd like that! Yesterday, she smiled at me … it was like someone had pulled out her teeth, soaked them in a mixture of rat droppings, baby puke and canal water, and then put them back in all mangled and crooked. Not a pretty sight to see, I can tell you!"

"Faz!" snapped Alfie. He had gone off on one of his rants, and volume was the only way to stop him. "I'm not talking about our dinner, lady!"

"Oh, you mean Mrs Fullylove. She must be older than a dinosaur by now. Not a pretty sight—"

"FAZ!" Alfie tried to compose himself and hide his nervousness. "I'm not talking about anyone who works here or teaches us. I'm talking about…new people… people who don't belong here…people who belong somewhere else…somewhere more dangerous. But for some reason these people are here…watching me."

Faz stared at Alfie with a look on his face that suggested his best friend had gone completely mad. "What's got into you? No-one is watching you because nothing exciting, or different, or interesting ever happens at this school. We wake up in the morning, put on our school uniform, and come to school; we lose at football and get ignored by everyone popular—and then we come home."

Faz struggled to his feet, "We are just ordinary people living ordinary lives, my friend—now come on, you mood hoover, we've got PE today!"

He would find another opportunity to find out the truth later.

Chapter 5

26 DAYS UNTIL MISSION

As the bell sounded, hundreds of children shuffled into the building and headed in different directions. As always, each child in Alfie's class was greeted at their classroom door by Mr Spencer, always with a warm smile.

"Morning, Alfie!" beamed his teacher, reaching out his hand for another of his vice-grip handshakes.

"Morning, Mr Spencer!" replied Alfie with clenched teeth.

"Morning, Fazioooo!"

"Good morning, Mr Spencer," replied a hesitant Faz, almost preparing for his hand to be crushed.

The two boys made their way to their seats over in the far corner of the room, both opening and closing their right hand in an attempt to regain the blood flow after the handshake. Mr Spencer had allowed them to sit together all year, even though he knew that they were best friends. Taking a reading book and sitting down, Alfie listened to the chorus of conversations on each of the five tables that were organised into the shape of a horseshoe, allowing for plenty of room for Mr Spencer to move around. One conversation in particular was louder than the rest and, unsurprisingly, it was being dominated by Connor Deangelo. "I mean, I'm the captain of the football team; I've got scouts from every club in the country watching me every week, and he has the nerve to say that to me in front of my parents! My father was threatening to go straight to the head teacher. No one has ever criticised me like that before, especially some stupid teacher!"

"So what did he say?" asked Ruby Samuels, who was practically the founding member of the Connor Deangelo fan club.

"He said… 'Connor took a theatrical deep breath in an attempt to gain further sympathy,'… I lacked resilience!"

"What? How can he think that? How can he say that?" said Michael Madison, another diehard member of 'Team Connor', who had no idea what resilience meant but was giving an Oscar-winning performance for his reaction, nonetheless.

"I mean," continued Connor, "it was me who won the cup for the school this year; it was me who scored the hat-trick in the final. Who else could've scored that winning goal when it was locked at 2-2?" The fan club all nodded in unison.

"And it didn't end there," continued Connor. "He started talking about my lack of empathy."

"What does Mr Spencer know about empathy, anyway?" exclaimed Freddie Draper, fan club member number three, who, at the same time, was trying to look up the dictionary definition of the word to gain an advantage over his rival members.

Alfie, who had been listening intently to every word, was desperately trying to hide his elation from Faz who, like Freddie Draper, was flicking excitedly through the dictionary. "Dictionary definition of resilience:" whispered Faz, "to be able to recover quickly from difficulty."

They both stared at each other.

"Dictionary definition of empathy: to understand and share the feelings of another."

Both boys shared a moment of silence; both considering the thoughts behind Mr Spencer's words. Connor had been almost untouchable at school. He was a gifted sportsman and the cleverest in the class in every subject. His tall, athletic frame gave him a natural confidence and his striking green eyes against his olive skin charmed teachers and children alike. But Alfie always noticed the way in which he treated his loyal friends: ordering them around, teasing them about personal things, and never allowing them to share any of the spotlight Connor received. Alfie had also remembered how Connor had acted during the only loss of the football season. Losing 3-0, Connor had refused to play and stood in the same spot on the pitch, firing insults at his team members, which included some being too fat and others too weak. Despite all of this, the football manager, Mr Long, had still refused to substitute him. Mr Spencer was right: he fell short on two of the MACER ingredients. Alfie - according to his teacher - had them all.

"Good Morning, you wonderful young people," spoke Mr Spencer, with his usual enthusiasm. The class fell silent. "A huge thank you to all who came to parents' evening last night, it was thoroughly enjoyable to meet and chat with intelligent people. And it was nice to talk to your parents too!" A ripple of laughter broke out from the children who understood the joke. "Now children, as you know, Friday afternoon means PE afternoon." There were a few fist pumps from some of the boys within the room. "Today's PE lesson will not be taking place in the school playground…it will in fact be at the local park." Confusion was etched across the faces of the thirty children. "I have arranged, with other local schools, to host a cross country race this afternoon…and everyone is taking part."

Mr Spencer sat in his chair, allowing for an eruption of chatter to fill the classroom. The information was met with mixed reviews. Lucy Bennett began telling everyone on her table how severe her asthma had become, even though she hadn't mentioned it once throughout the year. Timothy West proudly announced that he'd gobbled three plates of spaghetti the previous evening so he was destined for victory due to his increased energy levels. Gemma Thorne was sharing her hair dilemma story, complaining that her locks became frizzy in the wind, and Connor Deangelo was telling his disciples that his father was the Italian record holder for the 1500metres.

Alfie, in contrast, was sat staring at Faz who had turned a funny shade of green. He couldn't help but remember what Mr Spencer had said at the parent meeting: 'An impressive quality that I have observed is his ability to run." Alfie looked up at Mr Spencer and realised that his teacher had been watching him. A smile spread across the face of the man sat at the front of the class, followed by a nod of the head.

It was going to be an interesting afternoon.

Chapter 6

Elmdon Park was similar to many parks within a big city—a beautiful open space filled with freshly cut grass that lifted even the darkest of moods. Tomorrow, the park would be calm and serene with families lazily walking dogs in the late afternoon sun, allowing their children to roam around and let their imaginations run free. But today it looked very different.

A rainbow of colour filled the park as hundreds of children gathered, proudly representing their school in the glorious sunshine. The dark, blood-red of Crawford Cross was dutifully following a stretching routine carried out by their over-enthusiastic teacher, who looked like he was directing traffic; the royal blue-and-white of the ever-successful Edgewater Lane were busily discussing final strategies; and the deep, mysterious purple of Valley Vale were analysing the opposition through a series of points and stares. All were in complete contrast to the vibrant green-and-yellow of Pleasant Grove who were approaching the arena, ready for battle. The excitement was infectious.

"There's going to be at least two hundred boys on that start line, Faz, and look at the size of them all," said Alfie, suddenly very aware of his limited height.

"PMA Alfie. Positive. Mental. Attitude. Panicking will not get you anywhere leading up to a race."

Faz had paid a visit to the local newsagents during lunchtime and bought a copy of 'Runners Paradise'. After studying the magazine word-for-word, he had returned with two pasta meals, four large bottles of water and a packet of jelly babies.

"Preparation for the big race has gone well, training partner: we have eaten our pre-race meal - ninety minutes before the start time, we are drinking plenty of water to hydrate, and here's a couple of jelly babies each for an energy rush." Faz began guzzling the water as if he had just returned from an expedition across the Sahara Desert. "And if all else fails, I've always got the eagle!"

Alfie's best friend was the proud owner of a gold coin given to him by his grandfather before he died. The coin was called 'The Double Eagle' and

Faz often spoke of its rarity and claimed it to be priceless. He dismissed any idea of ever selling his most prized possession due to its sentimental value, but also, according to Faz, it blessed him with good fortune. Any success: video games, sporting activities, school tests – it was all down to The Double Eagle. Faz even claimed that the coin made him more attractive to girls. "They just can't stop staring at me when the eagle is in the pocket," he would often claim. Faz was right: girls did stare at him, but only because his stare was ten-times wider and ten-times longer.

"Boys to the start line, please," came the announcement from the over enthusiastic teacher, who was wearing an all-in-one tracksuit matching his school's colours, "boys to the start line, NOW!"

Alfie swallowed; butterflies began somersaulting like Olympic gymnasts in his stomach. The boys from the four schools made their way slowly to the designated area, all attempting to conserve their energy.

"Remember what I told you earlier, Alfie. Let's stick to our race strategy: the beginning of the race is all about maintaining a good pace." Alfie was amazed at how Faz could memorise information.

"Many of the runners will sprint at the start—it's a natural instinct. But they'll regret it later as their lactic acid levels increase."

"What's lactic acid?"

"I have no idea," admitted Faz, "but it said that on page 42. We must save something for the sprint finish; that is where the race is won or lost."

The instructions were clear: four orange cones marked out a rectangular course. Two laps of the course would determine the winner. Mr Tracksuit was doing everything in his power to build the tension, but the tension was already in the air. Hundreds of boys shuffled at the start line, attempting to find the perfect position, to make the perfect start.

"On your marks…"

Alfie lowered his body to allow him to shoot forward.

"Get set…"

He was alert for the next sound…

"GO!"

An army of boys bolted forward at a blistering pace, led almost effortlessly by Connor. Faz's prediction about the start had been correct.

Maintain a good race pace.

Alfie jostled for position right in the middle of

the chasing pack, who were now panicked and erratic. He focused on trying to find the right pathway, which forced him onto his tiptoes as if trying to avoid puddles in the rain. Rest-bite was found on the outside of the pack which allowed him to run more freely. He now had a better view of the front runners who were beginning to pull away— around a dozen of them desperately trying to stay with the leader, Connor Deangelo. Halfway through the first lap and Alfie had it all to do.

Panicking will not get you anywhere.

Alfie's attempts to increase his race pace were suddenly obstructed by a heavy fall within the stampede he had just moved away from. Faz, along with around ten other competitors, had fallen on top of each other like a collapsed rugby scrum. Many had gotten to their feet and continued with the race, but Alfie could see that Faz remained on the floor and was in some discomfort. Instinctively, Alfie headed back to where his best friend lay. Faz was clutching his ankle and writhing around on the floor in agony. Alfie realised his decision to help his friend would more than likely cost him the race, but he had to know if his training partner was alright.

"Faz, look at me!" instructed Alfie.

Faz opened his eyes, which had been tightly shut in an attempt to block out the pain. It took him a few seconds to recognise the face that was staring down at him. "Man down Alfie, man down!" strained Faz, struggling to catch his breath. "Race strategy… has gone out of the window!"

Alfie began to help Faz to his feet, but his large frame made it very difficult, forcing him to use energy that he would need for later in the race.

"Are you ok, partner?" asked Alfie.

"No!" snapped Faz, now very aware and angry. "You're wasting time with me when you should be at the front, making life hell for Connor! Go and win this for us; pick up your race pace and get yourself back into contention. But leave something for the end. GO!"

Following the instruction immediately, Alfie shot forward and assessed the impending situation. His first task was to catch the chasing pack, ideally by the end of the first lap. The gap to the leaders was considerable, but Alfie needed to take the race a step at a time. Crowds of people began to cheer after seeing his act of kindness with Faz, and this spurred him on as he passed Mr Spencer, who was standing on the third cone.

"Behind every set back is an opportunity,

Alfie!" Mr Spencer instructed. "Increase your race pace but stay relaxed!"

His legs kicked again in the direction of cone four, and he began concentrating on his breathing and relaxed his whole body to maintain his new speed. Gradually, the gap to the chasing pack began to close. By the end of the first lap, Alfie had caught and passed the pack of boys and was now out on his own. He felt strong.

Now it was time to focus on the leaders. The breakaway group, who now looked like tiny ants, were beginning to scatter as certain competitors began to tire. Alfie could see the leader, dressed in his own school colours of green and yellow, beginning to open up a gap from the rest, but perhaps not running as freely as before.

Their lactic acid levels will increase.

A surge of energy flooded his body as he kicked again, finding another gear.

Alfie had once read a book about a famous long-distance runner who had won a number of cross-country world titles. The book described each race as having uphill and downhill sections. Alfie couldn't remember his name but had never forgotten his answer to the question about his success.

"I would wait until the uphill section and smash it! Digging deeper than the rest is the key to success!"

Alfie had been so impressed by these comments that he had spent many of the following Saturdays running up a steep hill in his local park. The hill had exhausted him at first, but the more he persevered, the better he became.

Digging deeper than the rest is the key to success.

As Alfie rounded the first corner of lap two, he was met by a steeper section that had clearly been one of the reasons for the drop in pace from the leaders.

Smash it!

Head down, Alfie dug his heels into the ground and charged up the steep incline of the hill. This was where the gap had to close. Once again, the crowd sensed his determination and cheered raucously. After reaching the top of the climb, the view Alfie had been anticipating was better than expected. A group of boys from Crawford Cross, who had failed to stay with the elite runners, were within a few metres and fading quickly.

Stay relaxed. Maintain the race pace.

Alfie joined the exhausted athletes and switched to a more comfortable pace. It was time to consider his next move. Half a lap remained, and three runners were now ahead of him. Second and third place were clearly in view and catchable, but the lead Connor had created for himself was impressive. Alfie felt his whole body beginning to ache as he closed the gap on the main contenders. If he could only catch them before reaching Mr Spencer, then it would give him enough time to reach Connor. Alfie was now on the heels of the third-place runner from Valley Vale and the boy in second from Edgewater Lane was slowing considerably. All three reached the luminous orange cone together and rounded the final bend. Alfie could barely hear Mr Spencer as the crowd roared his name thunderously. But Alfie needed to hear his words.

"This is your moment, Alfie. This is your time. Catch him!"

The words surged through his veins, temporarily freeing him of any pain. He kicked for the finish at full speed, driving his arms and legs forward.

10 metres from the line.

Panicking, Connor began desperately looking behind him, causing his running style to become uncoordinated. His disbelief at how the race was unfolding was clear for everyone to see.

5 metres from the line.

Alfie was clawing back ground on the leader, but the gap to the finishing line was becoming ever closer. Pain had returned with a vengeance as every muscle in his body, starved of oxygen, felt like they were being stabbed by a thousand needles.

3 metres from the line … 2 metres from the line …

Clenching his teeth to deal with the agonising pain, he dragged himself level with Connor.

1 metre from the line.

Alfie threw himself over the line with every ounce of energy he had left. The momentum caused him to lose his balance as he crashed onto the floor, with Connor falling over him. Both runners lay on the floor, panting for breath. Too tired to move. Too tired to find out the final result. The race was over.

Chapter 7

Alfie hauled himself to his feet after what seemed like a very long time. His vision was blurry from sheer exhaustion, but he was able to make out Connor, who was now surrounded by his group of adoring followers. Ruby Samuels was busily checking his temperature by pressing the palm of her hand against his forehead, while Michael Madison was supportively patting him on the back as if he was choking on a chicken bone.

The four teachers from each of the schools were also huddled together, locked in conversation about something that seemed very important— perhaps the decision of who had actually won the race. But Alfie was much more concerned about another matter that was plaguing his mind: Faz.

A huge cheer from the crowd put an immediate end to his worries. Every spectator in the park was applauding, the only runner yet to complete the race. Alfie forced his way to the front of the now packed stand as Faz made his way tortuously to the finish line. Every painstaking step was met with yet another grimace on his sweat-covered face as his injured leg dragged behind him. But Alfie knew his best friend well; he knew that giving up would not be an option. Faz had always wanted the recognition of others, and now he was finally receiving it through an act of bravery that had encapsulated everybody. Alfie had never been so proud of his friend.

Faz crossed the finish line to a final, even louder round of applause and immediately collapsed into a heap. Before Alfie could attend to Faz, Mr Spencer appeared and diverted him over to where Connor and another runner from Edgewater Lane were standing. The runner, dressed in the royal blue-and-white of his school colours, shook Alfie's hand and congratulated him on his performance. The only thing Connor offered, in comparison, was an ice-cold stare of pure hatred. Delighted, Alfie knew his description of the bewildered Connor would cheer up his injured friend, but only after he knew the final result.

"If I could have your attention, please," spoke Mr Spencer, his words having the same effect on the spectators as it did on his class. "I know I speak on behalf of everybody here when I say what a captivating and spectacular race we have witnessed today." A chorus of agreement followed the comment, along with yet another round of applause. Mr Spencer waited patiently for the conversations and applause to naturally reach its conclusion. "It is my duty to announce the final positions. I apologise for the delay in proceedings but the battle for first place came down to the wire – a photo finish is what I think the professionals call it on television."

The moment had arrived.

"The winner of the Inter-City boys' cross-country race, is …"

The crowd fell silent. The longer the pause continued, the more Alfie questioned whether he had crossed the line before his rival competitor: had he timed his final lunge, right? Had he even drawn level with his opponent in the closing few metres? He pictured Connor being congratulated by Michael Madison earlier and realised that he must be the winner. How on earth could Alfie Andrews ever beat the unrivalled Connor Deangelo? He would settle for second place; it would be a huge achievement. He could go back to his life, living in the shadows of the likes of Connor…

"Alfie Andrews!"

Hundreds of pairs of eyes became locked on Alfie, all witnessing his look of utter astonishment.

He had expected this moment to be different. He had a vision of himself collapsing onto his knees with his hands hoisted in the air, looking up to the sky at the great athletes from the past looking down on him. He would then perform a victory lap with a golden medal around his neck, kissing his hands before releasing it into the air. Instead, he remained in the same spot, wearing the same awkward expression on his face. The crowd did their best to show they were pleased with the result: some began chanting Alfie's name, others began shaking his hand. One rather large man even ruffled his hair, causing his blonde locks to cover his eyes.

He simply didn't know how to react. After all, he had never won anything before.

"A smile would be a good start, Alfie," said Mr Spencer, appearing next to him.

"I'm sorry Sir. I'm just not used to...this…"

"Don't worry Alfie...sometimes special moments are enjoyed more when we look back on them."

Alfie saw the crowds begin to disperse,

allowing him to see Faz sat alone underneath an overhanging tree.

"He has taken it rather badly," said Mr Spencer, as they both stared at the deflated figure. "Right now, he needs his best friend."

Mr Spencer walked away and stopped.

"Oh, and Alfie… it really was a special moment."

Faz was picking up blades of grass and releasing them to watch their flight as they caught in the wind. It was clear that his real thoughts lay elsewhere.

"You know, it could be a lot worse…" said Alfie, approaching his friend.

"I finish in last place - thirty seconds behind the rest. I cross the line looking more like a zombie from an apocalypse film, and you say it could be worse?"

"It could," Alfie persisted. "You could be Connor and lead for the entire race right up until the finish…and lose to a nobody like me. I probably hadn't even entered his thoughts before today!"

Faz looked for the first time at Alfie, breaking into a smile. "I bet he was fuming at the end!"

"You should've seen his face when we were

waiting for the final result...he was firing daggers across the crowd at me. It was more awkward than watching my mum trying to flirt with Mr Spencer." Both boys burst out laughing at the vision of Connor experiencing failure for perhaps the first time in his life. "Besides," said Alfie, "you got the best cheer of the day."

"They felt sorry for me."

"They admired you! How many people would finish that race with that injury? No-one."

Faz smiled. "Well done anyway, mate. I knew you could win!"

"Couldn't have done it without your tactics."

"I'm more of a coach than an athlete. And anyway, I left the eagle in my trouser pocket—so that's the real reason! Need a lift? My mum's picking me up and taking me to A and E."

Alfie considered the question. His entire body was beginning to stiffen up and the thought of walking home was not appealing. He looked around at the now deserted park. A thought entered his mind.

"No. I think I'll walk. Anyway, you need to go straight to the hospital; you'll have to wait for a few hours."

"Please yourself," replied Faz. "Drink plenty

of water before you go to bed—it will help with the aching. Page 54. See you later, champ!"

Alfie watched his friend hobble away. Two cars were left in the car park: one was driven by Mrs Abbass, who was waiting to take her son to the hospital; the other, a black BMW with tinted windows, was occupied by two smartly dressed men wearing dark sunglasses. Once again, they had been watching him the whole time. The first car reversed and exited the car park. Without taking his eyes off the second car, Alfie opened the front section of his bag and took out the piece of paper. Satisfied, the black BMW roared into life and drove off into the distance.

Alfie's eyes finally rested on the page.

Chapter 8

Operation Andrews

Observation Process – General Information

Name: Candidate Andrews (C23)

Observation Duration: 17 days

Eye-Ball Time: 43 hours

Predicted Fitness Level: EXCEPTIONAL

Main Report

Section 1—In the 17 days of observation, Candidate Andrews has experienced success on three occasions: Parents' Evening, Working Wall, Cross Country Race.

He has not flaunted his achievements with any of his peers. REPEAT. He has not boasted about his success.

Mission Objectives—Candidate Andrews does not possess any egotistical qualities. His personality suggests he will maintain the secrecy of The Organisation.

Rating: EXCEPTIONAL

Section 2—Candidate Andrews has shown impressive results:

Average Top Speed (AST): 13mph.

Predicted Duration of Intensive Running (PDIR): 45 minutes.

These are some of the best results ever recorded during the observation period.

Mission Objectives: Candidate Andrews has the ability to escape any danger at speed and can maintain an increased pace for an extended period of time.

Basically, he can run like the wind.

Rating: EXCEPTIONAL

Section 3—No evidence has been gathered to determine his capabilities for section 3. This will be further explored during the application process.

Mission Objectives: How will Candidate Andrews cope when faced with the mission target?

Rating: INCONCLUSIVE

<u>Section 4</u> - Candidate Andrews has a close friendship with a Mr Faz Abbass. After completing the cross-country race, C23 showed a greater concern for the well-being of his friend than his own performance.

Mission Objectives: C23 will have no problem being sent on a joint mission. His personality suggests he will show loyalty to his partner and The Organisation.

Rating: EXCEPTIONAL

<u>Section 5</u>—Victory in the cross-country race was far from simple - much to the credit of Candidate Andrews. C23 was side-tracked from the race to attend to his injured friend. This cost C23 twenty-nine seconds and nearly the race.

Mission Objectives: When the mission reaches certain levels of danger and uncertainty, it is likely that Candidate Andrews will persevere.

Rating: EXCEPTIONAL

Further Information—Scare Level (SL) will be explored further during the application process.

Final Rating: PASS

Chapter 9

12 DAYS UNTIL MISSION

Alfie had forgotten how many times he had read the information on the piece of paper in the two weeks that followed the cross-country race. He had used every possible chance to study it just one more time. Mrs Fullylove's Maths lessons were usually a good opportunity as her eyesight did not travel as far as the back of the room. The dinner hall was another ideal spot. The potent fumes coming from his lunchbox—most recently a trio of crushed sprouts, boiled cabbage and fish paste—usually kept any potential visitors away.

At home, Alfie would lock himself in the toilet for hours to find peace from his mother, who was continually questioning him about the availability of Mr Spencer. This hideout was only ruined when Mrs Andrews had threatened to call the doctor about Alfie's 'number 2' issues.

The more he read, the more he questioned.

Why hadn't he seen the two men since the race? WHO and WHAT was The Organisation? And what on earth did 'Scare Level' mean?

Alfie did know one thing for sure: the two men were professionals. The information had been guarded very carefully throughout the day of the race, yet the men had clearly recovered the piece of paper and completed the report before returning it to the safety of his school bag.

But why?

Another message was clear: this process was far from over. The seventeen-day period where his life had been invaded was clearly known as 'The Observation Period'. Up next was 'The Application Process'.

But when would this begin?

Life after the race had returned to normal rather quickly. Alfie enjoyed the first few days when he had received endless compliments from everyone at school—apart from Connor and his small army of followers. In fact, Connor seemed to react so badly to Alfie's newfound attention that on the fourth day, Alfie felt a rather aggressive tap on his shoulder.

"I thought I'd join everyone else in congratulating you on your victory last week…" announced Connor insincerely, and loud enough for everyone to hear.

"Thanks," replied Alfie, who now realised he was completely surrounded by the Connor clan.

"You do realise I'd been injured leading up to the race…" continued Connor.

"Really? I had no idea!" Alfie wondered how long he'd been planning this speech.

"I pulled my hamstring during academy football training the evening before. My coach advised me against running, but I did it for the love of my school."

"Wow! You really are a true athlete, Connor," said Alfie, making no attempt to hide his sarcasm.

"Anyway, I just wanted to share my congratulations. It certainly was a surprise when someone like you finished the race ahead of someone like me—even if I did slip at the finish. Give the injury a month and I'll be back to full fitness." Alfie made an attempt to move away from his pack of wolves. "You know, my father had a similar problem to mine…" Connor was now addressing everyone. "My father—I'm not sure I told you—used to play football for Italy."

Alfie had been told. Many times.

"Unfortunately, my father suffered a terrible injury, landing awkwardly following a beautifully timed overhead-kick. Sidelined for three months, my father, the star striker, allowed his…understudy to play in his position. He allowed him to experience what it was like to be the great Giuseppe Deangelo."

Connor now faced Alfie once more. "You, Alfie, are like my understudy, keeping first place nice and warm before my return from injury."

Alfie thought Connor was going to hold out his hand to allow Alfie to kiss it, but instead the brainwashed group surrounding him began to chant 'Alfie, the understudy, Alfie, the understudy,' shooting devilish glares at anyone who didn't join in.

Faz, on the other hand, was totally unaware of the tension between Connor and Alfie. He had spent the following two weeks enjoying his newfound fame after his act of bravery in completing the race. Children throughout the school were desperate to hear his story and the more encouragement he was given, the more he exaggerated the truth. His latest account, witnessed by Alfie, was to a group of younger children in the school library. He explained that his kneecap had been tragically dislocated due to a butterfly-twist kick by a rival competitor, who happened to be a Kung Fu master. His high pain threshold had allowed him to reposition his deformed patella and complete the race; his unique healing powers meant that he only needed crutches for a period of two days. His description of the cracking sound at the point of impact was a step too far and made the smallest girl in the group scream with horror and run away in tears. His actual injury was a bruised knee, and he was sent home with a lollipop for being brave.

*

The summer holidays were approaching fast. Alfie was sat in a computing lesson on a Thursday afternoon with the task of researching the wildlife of the Amazon rainforest. Faz was happily quoting all the facts he had found in the thirty-minute activity, which proved to be rather off-putting to Alfie and the rest of the children on his table. Mr Spencer was busy sharing one of his fascinating stories about a recent adventure to the Amazon. The children on his table were scribbling down notes as if he was more knowledgeable than google.

Alfie, in comparison, was bored. The glory of winning the race was fading rapidly and the presence of the two men, which added excitement to his life, was a distant memory.

"Check this out!" exclaimed Faz, for what seemed like the hundredth time. "The Amazon is home to flesh-eating piranhas, and it says here that around 300 piranhas can rip the flesh off a human in less than five minutes. Not a pretty sight! I would chuck Mrs Lafferty in to see her wriggle around in agony. Her smell would probably put them off, don't you think, Alfie?"

Alfie, resting his chin in his hands, muttered a few words of acknowledgement without taking his eyes off his screen; it had suddenly gone blank and turned into a deep shade of blue. Words appeared on the screen in prominent yellow:

Alfie Andrews…

Is anyone looking at your screen?

Alfie's eyes darted around the room in every direction before resting in their original position. An answer was required.

No.

What you are about to read is strictly confidential. Do

you understand?

Alfie's heart began pounding as if trying to escape his chest. He glanced to his left. Faz was engrossed in his research.

Yes.

The observation period has been completed by two members of The Organisation. Are you aware of this?

Yes.

Is anyone else aware of this?

No.

Alfie had never withheld any information from his best friend in the seven years they had known each other. He had felt very uncomfortable hiding something so important. They had shared so many secrets and experienced so many things together.

The observation period was successful.

"Check this out!" Alfie angled his screen away from the predatory eyes of Faz and pretended to listen to his next fact. If he didn't give Faz his full attention, his best friend would wonder what was more important on his screen. Alfie needed to keep the information hidden. "Over 50 tribes living in the Amazon have never had contact with the outside world. Look at everything they're missing out on: mobile phones, computer games, football on every channel. I bet they haven't even tasted pizza. Can you imagine a life without pizza? The tomato base, melted cheese…"

The Organisation would like to ask you a question…

"… A choice of toppings on the menu: pepperoni, chicken, ham. I love pineapple on my pizza; I know it's controversial, but I stand by my decision as a valued customer."

The answer to this question will determine The Organisation's next move…

Alfie wanted nothing more than to be alone in a darkened room so he could concentrate fully on the sudden turn of events. Thankfully, Faz ended his rant and moved on to finding the next fact.

How would you feel about carrying out a mission on behalf of The Organisation?

Alfie considered the words to his answer very carefully. The answer, he thought, would change his life.

I would be interested.

The mission is potentially very dangerous. How do you feel now?

Excited.

The words on the screen disappeared, and he was once again left with the blue glow of the blank screen. He waited…

Letters began to appear at an increased rate. This time a much longer and final message.

The mission briefing will take place over the summer holiday period on Friday 5th August. You will be collected from your holiday accommodation at 23:55 and driven to our headquarters.

The secrecy of this mission and the existence of The Organisation is critical. This is the single most important piece of information you will receive. The Organisation is based on trust.

DO NOT SHARE THIS INFORMATION WITH ANYONE.

Until next time, Alfie Andrews…

Chapter 10

3 DAYS UNTIL MISSION

Ever since Alfie could remember, the three members of the Andrews' family would share a cottage in the middle of nowhere for a week during the summer holiday. Mrs Andrews, who was largely responsible for the annual adventure, described it as 'quality time'. In reality, Mr Andrews would continue to manage his overworked employees through his mobile phone, and Mrs Andrews would use the holiday as an excuse to sample the local wines at the nearest country pub, turning the place into a karaoke venue—much to the astonishment of the locals. The only thing that would prevent Mr and Mrs Andrews from their own individual 'quality time' was, of course, Alfie. This was solved by recruiting a new family member for the holiday period: Faz.

At midday on the 5th of August, the four

holidaymakers settled into Mr Andrew's range rover, which was about the size of his ego, and headed in the direction of the Lake District.

The journey was a complete disaster. Faz had prepared a list of travel games he had invented and proceeded to drive Mr and Mrs Andrews up the wall as opposed to up the motorway. First was the game 'name that tune' which involved Faz screeching out a song at full volume with the hope of someone guessing correctly. Fortunately for the rest of the passengers in the car, the game ended quickly, as nobody was able to guess his rather tuneless versions. Mrs Andrews did enjoy the next game of naming as many celebrities as possible in a minute. This gave her the opportunity to share her knowledge of male celebrities under the age of thirty who looked rather similar to Mr Spencer. Mr Andrews finally flipped when Faz suggested the challenge of creating the most annoying sound and within minutes, they were parked outside a service station.

13:55 – Ten hours remaining.

Mr Andrews, mobile phone pressed against his ear, headed in the direction of the nearest café; Mrs Andrews went straight to the ladies to reapply her fading lipstick; Faz shuffled over to a tiny arcade whilst digging out a handful of loose change. Alfie simply stood by the entrance and observed. He knew they were here. He could feel their eyes on him. Just like the day of the race.

And then they appeared.

They advanced through the crowds in the direction of Alfie, making no attempt to negotiate a pathway. People just moved out of their way subconsciously. They commanded respect so dominantly that you couldn't help but admire them. Today they were both wearing a brilliant yellow tie that cheered up their matching black shirts like a light bulb illuminating a darkened room. Their tailored trousers, the colour of brilliant blue, rested effortlessly on a pair of expensive Italian shoes. Without eye contact or a change in movement, the two men approached Alfie… and then walked straight past and out of the building. Alfie realised that his whole body had tensed up. As he relaxed, he could suddenly feel something in his pocket that hadn't been there before. He reached in and pulled out what looked like a present wrapped in a piece of light blue cotton, held together with yellow string.

"Just spent seven quid trying to win a teddy

with one of those stupid claw things," announced Faz, whose ability to appear at the wrong time was now at expert level. "Probably could've bought it for a quid at the pound shop, but it's the thrill of the chase that keeps me going. What've you got there?"

"Nothing," responded Alfie, hiding the object and immediately pulling out some change from his pocket. "I've got two pounds here. Don't let it defeat you!"

His spirit rejuvenated, Faz disappeared into the crowd for another shot at the prize.

Alfie carefully pulled the string apart and unfolded the cotton. Inside was what looked like a miniature torch with a message:

Leave your accommodation and follow the pathway down to the road. Press the button on the laser to indicate you have arrived.

23:55. Do not be late and come alone.

15:55 – Eight hours remaining.

"Look at this place! I bet it's haunted; it looks about a million years old!" Faz exclaimed, as he ran around the living room of their new home, changing direction at will.

Mr Andrews shuffled in behind him carrying as many suitcases that was humanly possible whilst pressing a mobile phone against his ear. Faz was right with his first observation: the room did look rather old. But it was impressive. A grand, log-burning fire was the centerpiece of the space with huge leather sofas carefully positioned, acting as the audience. Large oak beams covered the low ceilings, adding to the comfort and cosiness of the room. A close and loving family, Alfie thought, would cherish their winter evenings here with the fire burning brightly and the huge lamps illuminating their family games.

Alfie made his way to the bedrooms, hoping for his own room for a smooth exit. This plan was abandoned after seeing two beds in one room. Faz excitedly darted past him and jumped awkwardly onto the furthest bed and stared up at the similar-looking beams. Alfie gratefully took the bed nearest to the door.

"This room looks like a cave. I bet we could find a secret button that would reveal a secret passageway in the walls. Like in a Hollywood film." Faz began tapping different parts of the stone wall, hoping for something to magically happen.

A roaring voice from the living room interrupted Faz from continuing his role as Indiana

Jones.

"THERE'S NO BLINKIN' Wi-Fi!"

The two boys broke into a fit of hysterics.

22:55—One hour remaining.

The rest of the day had gone painstakingly slowly. Alfie and Faz had spent the afternoon at Lake Windermere, enjoying the breath-taking views by skimming stones across the rippling water. Faz proved to be a naturally talented skimmer. He was able to make his carefully selected stones almost water-ski across the lake at a blistering, splash-free speed and land exactly where he had predicted. He then spent an hour explaining to Alfie that his accuracy was the result of his world-class fielding skills in cricket and, of course, his lucky coin. He then announced that he would start a stone skimming club back at school in September until he realised there were no decent-sized lakes.

Mr Andrews had spent his time contacting the owners of the cottage to complain about the limited Wi-Fi availability, and Mrs Andrews had gone shopping, returning with enough wine to keep every pub in the Lake District going until Christmas.

With precisely an hour before the pickup time, Alfie's parents had stumbled drunkenly to bed, and the boys were in their room, and both were wide awake.

"I'm really shattered, Faz," said Alfie with an exaggerated, fake yawn, "maybe we should sleep and be fresh for a day of exploring tomorrow."

"But I feel like we haven't had a proper chat today?"

"Faz, we have spent every minute of the day together—you even stayed at mine last night!"

"I know, it's just this place—it's so exciting! It's so different to back home… lots of open space and not many people… I bet there's loads of stuff that goes on here at night… you could murder someone, and the police would never find out. I reckon the locals turn someone, zombies after midnight and go round looking for flesh to feed on."

Alfie swallowed. What was this mission that awaited him? "I'm going to sleep… and maybe tomorrow you can tell me more about these theories."

Alfie turned his body away from his best friend and waited nervously for the irritating sound of snoring. Tonight, it would be a welcome relief.

23:45—Ten minutes remaining.

Faz had been snoring long enough for Alfie to

be confident he was in a deep sleep. He slipped out of bed and removed his pyjamas, revealing black t-shirt and black combat trousers. He began lacing up his recently purchased army boots and tiptoed out of the room. The glow of the weakening fire added just enough light to guide him towards the door.

Alfie stepped out into the night. The brilliant moon provided comfort from the unwelcoming deathly blackness that surrounded him. He took a deep breath in an attempt to dissolve the nerves and reluctantly made his way down the pathway, towards the road…

Chapter 11

2 DAYS UNTIL MISSION

The road was deserted. He had expected streetlamps or even a few cars driving past, but he was once again encircled by darkness. Following instructions, Alfie pulled out the device and aimed it towards the road. He pressed the button and a dazzling yellow-and-blue laser shot through the night.

He waited…

Headlights suddenly flooded the road with brightness. Alfie took this as a signal and began to walk gingerly towards the vehicle. The black tinted windows made it impossible to see who was inside. The rear door opened by itself as he neared, and Alfie stepped in. Darkness greeted him once again. He could just make out the two huge silhouettes sat in the front seats.

"Put this on," instructed the driver, handing

him a blindfold without turning around.

Reluctantly, Alfie placed the mask on his face and was met by an overwhelming blackness. The engine started, and the car began to move.

"Where are we going…? How long is the journey…? Are you the two men who have been watching me…? What is this mission…?"

Silence filled the space required for each answer. The only thoughts that would be shared were his own. One thought dominated his mind…

What on earth have you gotten yourself into, Alfie?

The journey was about an hour. Alfie could hear the tyres crunching on gravel stones as the vehicle came to a standstill. He stepped out of the car and was led away by the two men. The ground surface underneath his feet quickly changed from rough to smooth, indicating they were now indoors. They continued to walk; the sound of heavy footsteps created an echo that broke the eerie silence. The footsteps slowed and three heavy thuds on a door made Alfie realise they had arrived at their destination. An attack of nausea flooded his throat, threatening to escape. The door opened, and he was positioned inside the room. His arms were released for the first time since getting out of the car and the footsteps belonging to the two men re-positioned themselves further inside.

"Take off the blindfold," spoke the same voice from before, deep with authority.

Alfie removed the mask. His eyes took time to adjust. The dimly lit room was vast in comparison to the amount of furniture. The same two men stood on either side of a huge oak desk with an unoccupied leather chair resting behind. A dominant chandelier hung from the ceiling as a constant reminder of the room's past.

Another door opened. A man appeared dressed elegantly in the same blue suit. This man was older. His close-cropped hair was immaculately kept and an expertly trimmed silver beard surrounded his slightly longer moustache, curled fabulously on either side. This man was the boss. He settled into his chair and addressed his guest with his piercing blue eyes.

"Welcome Alfie," came a well-spoken, velvety voice. "Allow me to introduce you to my colleagues. I would imagine you have grown rather curious of these two gentlemen. This is Rockwell to my left and McKenzie to my right."

Both men nodded.

"You are also curious—I'm sure—as to why

you are here and why we have landed in your world."

Alfie attempted to say 'yes' but no sound came out.

"We are a secretive government organisation known simply as 'The Organisation'. Nobody knows we exist apart from high-ranking members of the government, including the Prime Minister and, of course, The Queen."

This still did not explain the reason why Alfie was stood in front of them.

"We specialise in cases that are a little out of the ordinary. Anything that the government wants to keep hidden away. People like to live their lives without fear."

Alfie glanced at the door the man had appeared through. He was completely out of his depth.

"You are here to assist us with our most recent mission," continued the man in charge. "We are attempting to track down the whereabouts of the person who is ranked number one on The Organisation's 'Most Wanted List'."

The blood drained from Alfie's face.

"His name is Cassian Duke. McKenzie, share his file with our new recruit."

"Cassian Duke was a former member of The Organisation." McKenzie's voice matched his appearance—deep and mountainous. "More commonly known as The Duke, he was a former SAS elite soldier. He's the best of the best: strong, fearless, a unique ability to think strategically under extreme pressure. A leader of men. Around eighteen months ago, on a mission in the Sahara Desert, The Duke vanished. We need to find him.

"What happened to him?" Alfie spoke for the first time.

"You will be informed when the time is right," said the man in charge.

The room fell silent. The silence lingered in the air. The man in charge was studying Alfie thoughtfully. Like the midnight pickup, like the car journey, and the blindfold, this was part of the application process. The Scare Level. Alfie didn't flinch.

"Have we made the correct choice?" asked the man in charge.

"Yes, Boss," came the response in perfect unison.

"Then there is one more thing you should know...Cassian Duke returned a completely different man. The Duke now has the potential to cause worldwide destruction." The man in charge looked even deeper into Alfie's eyes. "He must be stopped."

His tone suddenly changed. "Forgive me for not introducing myself...My name is Bruce Spencer, and we have named this mission 'Operation MACER'."

Chapter 12

"Hello Alfie." Mr Spencer appeared through the same door as his father.

"I believe you are slightly more familiar with our fourth member of The Organisation," said Bruce Spencer, wearing a delicate smile.

"Alfie, you have been under observation since the beginning of the school year." Mr Spencer made his way further into the room, the light revealing a similar blue suit to the others. The likeness between father and son was noticeable: that same aura of superiority. "I assumed the role of your class teacher in order to find and recruit a suitable candidate for this mission … you have been chosen."

"One of the best reports I've ever written," announced McKenzie.

"Oh, agreed!" said Bruce Spencer. "Your empathy section was a fascinating read."

"Athleticism was outstanding as well, boss.

The boy can run," added Rockwell, confirming the report.

Everything was now beginning to fit into place, like the final jigsaw piece of a puzzle. Each section of the report represented an element of MACER. Why hadn't he connected the report to the comments made by Mr Spencer at parents' evening? Mr Spencer was adored by all of the children at his school—including Alfie. Teachers were not supposed to be adored. Faz would often joke that all teachers turned into robots the minute they qualified. Their own mission was to deliver dull lessons wearing even duller clothes; their objective to suck the life out of children through a combination of droning voices and suffocating coffee fumes. Mr Spencer was completely different. But Mr Spencer wasn't a teacher; he was part of the most secretive organisation in the country— perhaps even the world.

"Your mission, Alfie Andrews…" spoke Bruce Spencer, "is to track down the whereabouts of the most wanted man in the history of this organisation and assist in eliminating him from his agenda. Do you accept?"

Alfie thought carefully about the words spoken by the leader. He had now composed himself rather well after seeing a familiar face. "I will accept as long as you answer some of my questions."

"Very well," responded Bruce Spencer, as if expecting the reply, "you have three."

Alfie quickly realised that he hadn't prepared any of these questions. He just knew he had many. The room fell silent and four of the most intimidating pairs of eyes rested on him.

"Why me?"

"You were the most suitable candidate!" replied Bruce Spencer immediately. "You have had your first question."

Alfie felt irritation rising up inside him. He had phrased the question incorrectly under pressure, and the existing members knew it. Not a great start to his new career. He tried again…

"You are four of the strongest men I have ever met, so why do you need… me to carry out your own mission?"

"Oh Alfie, you're making me blush!" said Rockwell, placing both arms out to the side and flexing his ginormous bicep muscles.

"Compliments will get you far in this club, kiddo. He's making a good impression, boss," added McKenzie.

"Good question, Alfie!" chuckled Bruce, his smile revealing a hint of kindness in his eyes. "It is now known to us that Cassian Duke possesses certain abilities that are beyond human. One of many is his ability to remain hidden. If our predictions are correct, you may be able to locate his whereabouts more successfully."

Alfie knew another question would be his third and final, so he stood in silence, hoping for more information…

Bruce Spencer smiled. "You are smarter than even the report suggests. So answer this … what are you,that we are not?"

Alfie knew the answer immediately. "I'm a child!"

The four men all smiled and nodded their approval like proud parents after their child had performed his first magic trick.

"Correct!" erupted Rockwell, both arms hoisted in the air.

"I think our new member is finally ready for his education, Damien," announced Bruce Spencer. "After all, you were his teacher for a year. Damien—sorry - Mr Spencer, will drive you back to your accommodation and brief you fully. Today's lesson: The History of Cassian Duke!"

Bruce Spencer stood and buttoned his jacket. "Until next time, Alfie Andrews!"

"You haven't allowed me to ask my final question...Sir?"

"Then ask…" said the boss.

"Why was I named C23?"

"Take it away Rockwell," replied Bruce Spencer as he turned and walked towards the exit, disappearing from view.

"Candidate 23, you were named after the number worn by a very famous basketball player – Michael Jordan."

"Why?"

"That's a fourth question!" countered Rockwell with a playful smile. "But I'll let it pass!"

The three remaining men stood staring at Alfie, waiting for his reaction to the answer.

"Because Michael Jordan was the best."

Chapter 13

The journey began in silence. Alfie needed time to consider the information that had been thrust upon him. Mr Spencer seemed to accept this and concentrated on steering the car in the direction of Lake Windermere. The engine purred deliciously, and the momentum of the car provided the comfort that Alfie needed.

"So what now?" he asked, fifteen minutes into the journey.

"I must convince you to accept the mission and arrange to collect you at 15:00 hours later today," said Mr Spencer. "We will discuss and agree a strategy to ensure that your family members—particularly Faz—are unaware of your absence. This may prove difficult."

Mr Spencer's honest and direct response was a welcoming relief to the unanswered questions of the past few weeks.

"Tell me about The Duke; I need to know

more."

Mr Spencer allowed a few moments to gather his thoughts.

"Cassian returned a completely different man—a shadow of his former self. Before his capture, The Duke was at the centre of everything. He was my father's most trusted and valuable soldier. The most dangerous and technically challenging missions were all carried out by Cassian - often completely alone. He was responsible also for the training of new recruits, including Rockwell and McKenzie. He was quite simply irreplaceable."

"Within days," continued Mr Spencer, "Cassian had isolated himself from the group, lost in his own dark thoughts. He rarely spoke and when he did, it was always negative: pain, suffering, death. One evening stood out in those few weeks following his return. We were based in a farmhouse up in Scotland, preparing for a mission after an unusual sighting near Loch Ness. It was the middle of the night—maybe three in the morning. I couldn't sleep, so I went to the kitchen for a glass of water. Cassian was sitting in complete darkness on the floor in the corner of the room. I approached him … his eyes were open … he was staring right through me … his head was moving … shaking almost … as if in some sort of trance. I attempted to release him from this spell he was under by shouting his name. And then he spoke. The words I will never forget…"

"What did he say?" asked Alfie, eager to know more.

'The darkness surrounds me. It suffocates my mind… it clouds my vision… it contaminates the oxygen I breathe. The darkness is beginning to take control…'

"The next day he was gone. Rockwell and McKenzie were relieved. My Father was concerned."

"So, he disappeared again?" Alfie asked.

Mr Spencer slowed the car considerably to make a sharp left before continuing the story.

"Our next mission was to investigate a small village in Northern Scotland. There had been a sudden change in behaviour of the residents. Not in appearance, but personality. They had all left their homes and were wandering around the village. It was as if their emotions had been removed: their faces were expressionless, they wandered aimlessly; no work had been completed, and no communication was shared. They had quite simply lost their purpose."

"Cassian?"

"We searched and searched for anyone who showed human emotion, careful not to come into contact with those affected. But it seemed all had fallen victim. Except one. A girl around your age was found hidden in the undergrowth around half a kilometre from the village centre. She was distressed, which signalled emotion. The story she shared was shocking."

"Skye had explained that a man had been turning locals into 'death walkers', including her own family—something the poor girl had witnessed before her escape. The man's stare was all it took. A stare that made his eyes light up like fire against the night sky. The men, women and children who returned the stare were never the same; it was as if their life had been sapped from them. That is the reason why this brave little girl named them 'death walkers.'"

"Skye provided us with a detailed description of the man responsible. Our worst fear was confirmed ... The man fitted the description of The Duke."

"Skye offered to lead us in the direction of

where Cassian was based, a derelict house on the other side of the village – a house that she had never seen before, which was unusual considering the town was so small and the girl was intelligent beyond her years. Cassian was nowhere to be found when we arrived. And nor was the house. We were looking at an empty space."

"She was lying?" suspected Alfie.

"Impossible," countered Mr Spencer. "Our advanced training allows us to detect a lie within the first ten seconds of a conversation; better than any test ever created. She was telling the truth."

"So, what happened?"

"We returned with Skye to our base to re-evaluate. Skye begged us to allow her to return to the deserted house alone, convinced that our presence was the reason for its disappearance. We refused. We left her in a separate room while we discussed new strategies. Within minutes, she had climbed out of a window and escaped."

"She went back to the house?"

"A field search was carried out by organisation members, led by Rockwell and McKenzie. My father and I remained at base, hoping she would return. We discussed her theory and realised it was the only theory. We sat in silence, completely helpless. My father suddenly jumped to his feet and selected two pairs of specialised magnification binoculars. I knew his plan immediately. These binoculars could allow us to see for miles. We focused on the location we had previously visited and could make out Skye staring at the empty space - only to her it wasn't an empty space. Only she could see the house; only she could see Cassian."

"That was the last we saw of her. She disappeared from view and the field search was unsuccessful. We failed to look after a young girl who had already experienced such misery. She deserved more …"

A single tear began to collect in the corner of each eye. Mr Spencer was still deeply affected by these events, and sharing the story once again was bringing everything back to the surface. He swallowed deeply.

"Of the seventy-nine residents, seventy-eight became death walkers. The Duke disappeared once again, along with six of the walkers, and has not been seen since. Seventy-two victims remain in the village, behaving in exactly the same way. Lower-ranking members of The Organisation now have the unfortunate job of keeping this a secret from the rest of the world. On a daily basis, they have to monitor a population of villagers who have had their life removed. These organisation members now only refer to Cassian as 'The Duke of Darkness'."

The car crawled to a standstill beside the path that led to the Andrews' holiday accommodation.

"We have chosen you, Alfie, because you remind us of Skye. In the short time we knew her, she was courageous and athletic, with a deep understanding of people's feelings. She was brilliantly determined yet humble. She was the reason why MACER was created. Only children who are blessed with these qualities can see through the venom he is attempting to cast upon the world. You, Alfie - our only hope - are blessed with these qualities also. You have to accept this mission."

Alfie glanced at his watch. It was approaching 5am and the first signs of daylight were greeting the horizon. Exhaustion was overpowering his entire body, yet his mind was active, racing with a mixture of thoughts. Accepting the mission would mean an immediate risk to his young life. Refusing the mission would mean a return to life before The Organisation. Before it became exciting. A series of images flashed into his mind. First, Connor and his followers chanting, 'Alfie, the understudy'. Then, the figure of his father glaring down at him, the familiar look of disappointment etched across his face. But it was the third image that was the most powerful. The image of a young girl searching in the darkness; lost, vulnerable, and completely alone. A girl who was once a daughter to a loving mother and father, only for it to be taken away by a man who needed to be stopped.

He turned to face his teacher, who was waiting for his response. "Mr Spencer, when the car arrives tomorrow at three o'clock … I will be waiting."

Chapter 14

1 DAY UNTIL MISSION

The bedroom was empty when Alfie woke. His eyes felt heavy from the previous evening and his aching body yearned for more sleep. The alarm clock next to his bed, glowing 10:33, warned against this, so he got up and stretched to ignite life into his tired muscles. The smell of a cooked breakfast floated temptingly into the room, causing his stomach to growl. A meal was exactly what he needed for the day ahead and Mrs Andrews, despite her peculiar sandwich choices, cooked a legendary fried breakfast.

The person wearing the apron and standing next to the frying pan when he arrived in the kitchen was not his mother; neither was the apron worn by his father—who actually wasn't a bad cook when he could tear himself away from his banking empire. The person, to Alfie's disbelief, wearing a pink apron with the words 'THIS CHICK DIGS COOKING' (written in diamond studs) was actually Faz.

"Morning sleepyhead. Thought I'd surprise my new family with a breakfast treat—and you're just in time!"

Mr and Mrs Andrews were sat at either end of the table in their dressing gowns, both wearing a worried expression.

"I was just telling Arthur and Maureen," explained Faz, "about how I've been watching that chef on TV—Gordon Whatshisface. He reckons you need to be creative in the kitchen, so I thought I'd do a cooked breakfast with a tropical twist!"

Alfie's appetite was fading rather quickly.

"So," Faz continued, pretending he actually was Gordon Ramsey and Alfie was the cameraman, "I've decided to fry the bacon in strawberry jam and soak the sausages in pineapple juice. The eggs are scrambling beautifully but I did drop half the egg shell in so there'll be a bit of a crunch!"

Reluctantly, Alfie joined his parents at the table and was served with a shrivelled plate of food that was swimming in a watery orange sauce. Faz sat there staring at his three guests, waiting for their approval. Alfie forced a forkful into his mouth and chewed hesitantly.

"Whadayathink?" asked Faz, through a mouthful of slop.

"Mmmmmmmm," replied Alfie and his mother together, while Mr Andrews battled a coughing fit that turned his face beetroot red.

It tasted like vomit that had travelled into your mouth before being re-swallowed.

"I've an action-packed day planned for us!" announced Faz, showering Alfie with bits of eggshell. "First up is a bike ride, followed by an assault course I found on the internet. We then relax with a late afternoon boat cruise across Lake Win—"

"Arthur, no mobile phones during mealtime!" snapped Mrs Andrews.

"This isn't a meal; I wouldn't feed this to the devil!"

"What was that, Arthur?" questioned Faz suspiciously.

"He said your food deserves a medal," explained Mrs Andrews, in an attempt to avoid upsetting the chef.

Faz Beamed.

"To be honest, Faz, I'm not feeling very well

today," Alfie fibbed. "I think I need to go back to bed."

"I'm not surprised after the food you ate!" said Mr Andrews.

"What?" questioned Faz.

"He said the food was great!" added Mrs Andrews, who was becoming rather flustered by her husband's rudeness.

"I've got an idea," plotted Alfie, looking at Faz. "How about you take my parents with you? It could be their way of saying thank you for the lovely breakfast you cooked!"

"But the food made me want to puke!" argued Mr Andrews.

"He said the food was fit for a Duke!" blurted Mrs Andrews in a state of panic.

The mention of the name made Alfie shudder.

"I think it's a wonderful idea!" announced Mrs Andrews over enthusiastically, in an attempt to make up for her husband once again.

"I need to be by the phone today," said Mr Andrews. "You carry on without me."

Mrs Andrews glared at her husband, making her eyes bulge out of her sockets like a cartoon character. "Arthur Andrews, this holiday is a chance to spend some time together as a family. Now, poor Alfie is unwell, but you are FINE. So, if you don't join us on our family day out, I WILL SHOVE THAT PHONE SO FAR UP YOUR BOTTOM, IT WILL BE POKING OUT OF YOUR MOUTH!"

Mr Andrews looked like a toddler who had just been refused a sweet.

"Just don't let him cook any food," he mumbled moodily. "It tasted like manure.

"Faz, my husband said he will gladly accept your invitation; that's for sure!"

*

There were two reasons why the journey to the headquarters was much more enjoyable: firstly, Alfie wasn't wearing a blindfold; and secondly, Rockwell and McKenzie had been in a more talkative mood. By the time the car pulled up an hour later, it was as if Alfie had known them his entire life:

Likes: eating steak (served rare); lifting very heavy weights in the gym; WWE wrestling (their finishing moves both sounded painful); playing chess (good for the mind); playing video games (good for coordination); musicals (Rockwell—The

Phantom of the Opera moved him to tears); flower arranging (McKenzie—the variety of colours always lifts his mood).

Dislikes: Death Walkers; Cassian Duke; Connor Deangelo. (This pleased Alfie).

The headquarters was a huge manor house consisting of countless rooms that spread across the impressive building. Parts of the house looked modern, with stone-washed white walls and eye-catching, black-framed windows. Other parts maintained their original features. Its dark windows against the aged red brickwork gave the place a sense of mystery—a sense of danger even. The old and new combination, along with the sheer size of the property, dominated Alfie's vision and tempted him inside.

The laughing and joking between the three mission members continued until they reached the meeting room. Rockwell and McKenzie quickly switched to professional mode, straightened their ties and entered. A circular table directly underneath the chandelier had been added to the furniture in the room. A chink of sunlight, appearing through a gap in the curtains, flooded the table with a spotlight of brightness.

"Take a seat, Alfie," instructed Rockwell.

Alfie sat at one of the five vacant seats and was joined by his travelling companions. Bruce and Damien Spencer appeared through the separate door, deep in conversation, and made their way over to the table. They all waited for Bruce Spencer to speak.

"You've had these two gentlemen stalking you for weeks; you've been dragged away blindfolded in the death of the night; you've been asked to find one of the most dangerous men in the world. And you are still here."

All eyes rested on Alfie; the three other men nodding their approval to the words spoken by their boss.

"I think we can safely say he passed the scare test, boss!" said Rockwell.

Further agreements were shared.

"Are you ready for this, young Alfie?" asked Bruce, clicking his pen repeatedly in anticipation.

"Under your guidance, I believe I am," came the reply.

Bruce smiled; his silver moustache curling even more on either side. "Well, in that case, we shall begin the mission briefing. Damien?"

"It is understood that The Duke has a new

base 30 miles north-east from here," explained Mr Spencer. "It is believed to be another house."

"How do you know this if you can't see the house?" asked Alfie dubiously.

Mr Spencer looked at his father, who nodded for him to continue.

"We have access to all police records across the country. One particular station received a call from a local resident about a house that had suddenly appeared."

"That could mean anything," said Alfie, growing in confidence.

"The caller claimed that it wasn't he who could see the house, it was his ten-year-old son."

"Stage one of the mission is fact-finding," said Bruce, taking over. "We want you to visit the location and gather as much information as you can. You will be fitted with a wireless earpiece so that Damien and I can communicate with you at all times. Rockwell and McKenzie will assist you on foot, but obviously they will have to keep their distance."

Alfie couldn't help but enjoy the fact that the two scariest men he had ever seen were going to be his assistants.

Bruce Spencer continued. "You will be driven by car and dropped off about a mile from the house," he said. "The rest of your journey will be on foot through a densely wooded area. When you arrive at an abandoned railway track, follow the route and you will reach the house."

"We just hope that it will appear for you," added Mr Spencer.

"Oh, it will appear for him," Bruce confirmed. "He's been well chosen."

The room fell silent. Rockwell and Mckenzie were checking their phones simultaneously and Mr Spencer was scribbling notes onto a piece of paper. Bruce Spencer's eyes remained on Alfie, examining every facial expression, searching for confirmation that he had, in fact, made the correct choice. Alfie felt hideously uncomfortable.

"Alfie," he spoke finally, "I want you to listen very carefully to this next instruction. DO NOT go within twenty metres of the house. Stage one is all about gathering basic information: What is the house like from the outside? Is he working alone? What are the entry and exit points? Your safety is our main concern."

The sound of a ringing telephone sliced through the final part of the instruction. Rockwell left the table and headed in the direction of his superior's desk.

"What did you say to your parents?" asked Mr Spencer, filling the silence.

"Told them I wasn't feeling very well, so they went out for the day with Faz," replied Alfie.

"Boss, phone call for you."

Bruce Spencer left to take the call, leaving his son in charge.

"Are they suspicious?" he probed. "The last thing we need is the local police searching for a missing boy."

"My room is dark," said Alfie. "My bed looks like somebody's sleeping in it, and a note is waiting in the kitchen explaining that I need to sleep off the projectile vomiting and severe diarrhoea. Even Faz won't come near me!"

Bruce returned from his phone call; a concerned look etched across his face. "That was Zebrisky on the phone. News from Scotland …"

The leader took a deep breath.

"In the past hour, the remaining death walkers have collapsed and died. Cassian is now responsible for the deaths of seventy-two people. This mission needs to begin. Immediately!"

Chapter 15

"Stay hidden at all times!" said Rockwell.

"Stay low; stay small; blend in; keep an irregular shape—move SLOWLY," said McKenzie.

"Watch out for puddles, gravel, crunching leaves, crackly sticks, rustling bushes," said Rockwell.

"Think about your breathing: slow and steady," said McKenzie.

"If you think you've been seen—STAY STILL," said both.

Alfie was being swivelled around from Rockwell to McKenzie like a ballroom dancer, listening to an onslaught of final instructions. He was now dressed from head to foot in a camouflaged army outfit, which included green-and-brown face paint, and was stood on the edge of the vast woodland he was about to enter.

"Do I get some sort of weapon?" he asked, becoming increasingly concerned that his only protection was a pair of sunglasses.

"The best weapon sits between your ears," answered Rockwell. He wasn't talking about the sunglasses. "Keep your mind sharp and you'll be perfectly safe—as long as you listen to the boss."

"I don't even know what The Duke looks like," Alfie protested.

"Trust me when I say this, Alfie…" replied McKenzie, a frown appearing on his face as if he was digging out a memory from the past. "You'll know. Just make sure you see him before he sees you."

"It's time," Rockwell announced.

Alfie's stomach dropped like he was on the pirate ship at a theme park. With a feeling of dread, he entered the emerald jungle. Rockwell and McKenzie's words chased each other around his brain as he instinctively adopted a crouched position, moving slowly and steadily forward.

The dense woodland was a beautiful site: the majestic trees were tall and dominant, glowing tenderly as the sunlight filtered through, casting shadows that danced to the rhythm of the wind. The air around was bright and cheerful, filled with a symphony of joyous birds. To his surprise, Alfie found himself enjoying the journey so much that he was soon lost in his own thoughts. He imagined that he was closely following the man he was tasked to find. Every few seconds, The Duke would spin around sensing an intruder, and Alfie would dart behind a tree or a thicket, waiting for the danger to pass. His game allowed him to move closer and closer to his target, forcing him to adapt his movements as the danger increased: crouching became crawling, tiptoeing overcame walking, and steady breathing was replaced with holding his breath. He was so preoccupied by his imagination that it took him a few moments to realise that a voice was speaking repeatedly in his ear.

"Alfie … Alfie … can you hear me? Why am I being told that you are crawling along the ground and hiding behind obstacles?" Bruce Spencer's questions pounded his ear drum.

"Just practising my movement techniques," fibbed Alfie, forgetting he was being watched by Rockwell and McKenzie and feeling a little embarrassed.

"You should be approaching the railway track now; this is where you need to start communicating with us, Alfie." Alfie detected a nervousness in the voice of his new boss.

"Will do, boss," he replied, in an attempt to reassure both Bruce and Mr Spencer.

Alfie arrived at the disused railway track. The rotting wooden beams were infected with clumps of moss, spreading like a deadly disease along the track. The mood of the forest had changed. A brooding mist began to overpower the handsome sun from earlier, silencing the singing birds and darkening Alfie's thoughts. Self-doubt crept back to the surface of his mind as he followed the track into the mist.

"Ok, boss, I'm now walking along the track." Alfie hoped the silky voice of Bruce Spencer would provide the comfort he needed.

"Good Alfie. Keep to the track until you see something. Remember, share as much as possible—we are here with you all the way!"

Alfie continued along the curve of the track tentatively, his vision obscured by the thickening mist. The feeling of unease was growing with every step. Every nerve in his body warned him not to go any further, but he knew aborting the mission was not an option.

Not now.

"I see something…" announced Alfie, his

heart escaping into his throat. His eyes scanned along a passage crowded either side with overhanging trees intertwined to form an archway. Stepping off the track for a better view, Alfie could make out a shape at the far end.

"What do you see, Alfie?" probed Bruce.

Alfie stood motionless, allowing his eyes to answer the question. The mist had faded slightly, but the thickness of the trees prevented any light from filtering through. Despite this, he knew the answer.

"The house."

Without waiting for a response, Alfie slipped effortlessly back into mission mode. He darted to his right and attempted to lose himself within the gnarled branches. Happy with his position, he edged forward.

"I will give you an eye-ball description when in position, over," Alfie spoke with a stern whisper.

Part of him couldn't wait to reach the end of the passage; part of him dreaded the thought. He continued, clearing his mind of negativity, concentrating on the approach without being seen. The experienced trees whispered words of warning in the wind as Alfie neared the clearing, crawling the final few metres.

"I'm in position."

"Excellent mission so far, Alfie." Mr Spencer was now in his ear. "Now, what do your eyes tell you?"

"It's a house on a lake."

Mr Spencer probed. "Exit and entry points?"

"You need to cross a bridge, otherwise you walk around the perimeter of the lake - which would take longer. A lot longer."

"How big is the house, Alfie?"

"Quite big."

"Be specific…"

"Erm … farmhouse size, four bedrooms, main entrance is front centre, there is a light on upstairs to the right."

"Anything else?"

"Death walkers."

"Why are they still alive?" Mr Spencer's voice was uncomfortable. "How many? Where?"

"Two guarding the bridge; two either side of the house; one guarding the main entrance. They are huge!"

"How big?"

"They make Rockwell and McKenzie look like children."

Alfie was hidden in the undergrowth, staring at the five giants. Rippling muscles had broken through their now undersized clothing. Their eyes, frog-like, were glowing intermittently; their mouths, wearing a lifeless expression, were unaware of the drool slobbering down their chins; their skin had sunken into their skeletal face. They were a terrifying sight.

"We only see Alfie and a lake, boss," confirmed Rockwell. "No bridge, no death walkers, and no house."

Alfie could hear Bruce Spencer now questioning his other mission members, building a picture in his mind, collecting the facts before making his next move - like a game of chess.

"Alfie, can you hear me?" asked Bruce.

Alfie responded without taking his eyes of the house. "Yes, boss."

"We want you to remain in the same position for one hour."

"An HOUR?"

"This time period will allow us to establish any routines taking place," explained Bruce Spencer, ignoring the surprise in Alfie's voice. "Do they rotate the guards? Where is the sixth death walker? Where is Cassian situated in the house? If anything changes Alfie, you must inform us immediately."

"What happens after an hour?"

"You leave and return to the drop-off point."

"But -"

"This is non-negotiable. This is stage one. We are fact finding. You will return. Is that understood?" There was a sharpness to Bruce Spencer's voice that Alfie hadn't heard before.

"Yes, Sir."

"Good. Sit tight Alfie, and keep us informed…"

Seconds felt like hours, minutes like days as Alfie waited in the same uncomfortable position, his face pressed into the dirt. Nothing had changed: the death walkers remained in the same position, and 'The Duke of Darkness' was living up to his name. The adrenaline from earlier had been replaced by a mixture of boredom and frustration. Alfie's thoughts wondered to his observation report. The only MACER category not to be given outstanding was Courage. He had been dragged into this world, risking his life for a group of individuals he barely knew. One minute he was a hero giving them information they desperately needed, and instead of being trusted to investigate further, and prove his outstanding courage, he was being ordered to observe and return to base.

He had been used.

But rules were created to be broken.

Chapter 16

Alfie's mind sprang into life. He needed a diversion for the death walkers.

"Build a fire!" spoke his first thought.

"I don't know how!" responded his rational mind.

"Throw a stone to smash a window," offered his second thought.

"I'd be lucky to reach the lake," came the logical response.

Alfie adjusted his position and felt something in his pocket.

Something he had kept with him from the previous day. His third thought was the best option ...

The archway of trees offered protection from the sunlight and acted as the perfect place to shine the laser beam. Alfie, belly to the ground, manoeuvred himself backwards to where the overhanging branches were more closely packed together. Carefully, he rested the laser beam onto a bed of leaves and clicked. A brilliant beam of yellow and blue light punctuated the air. Five pairs of enlarged hypnotised eyes fixated on the glow.

Spellbound, the guards advanced forward: their movements were awkward, as if still struggling to adjust to their new size. Alfie skilfully shuffled back to his original position, waiting for the right moment.

Still, the death walkers lumbered forward, four of them now forming a defensive line. Alfie just needed the fifth walker to make his final few steps off the bridge …

"ALFIE! Why is your laser beam on? Repeat, why has your laser beam been activated?" Bruce Spencer's voice had lost its poise and was splintered with panic.

Ignoring his superior, Alfie thundered forward, springing through the air like a long jumper. He landed expertly on the bridge, maintaining his speed as he crossed the wooden panels at a blistering pace. He collapsed to the side of the main entrance, twisting his body to check the position of the death walkers. They were still inspecting the radiance of the light. Instructions pounded his ear, both father and son demanding him to retreat. But it was too late. Alfie removed the communication device, stuffed it into his pocket, and reached for the door handle. It opened with a heavy creak and Alfie slipped inside.

The entrance hall was different to what he had expected. His feet sunk into a magnificent red carpet that covered the floor and travelled up an inviting central staircase. The route to the first floor was illuminated by a huge pair of candlesticks that stood as guards at the foot of the stairs. Darkness filled the rest of the space. The four corners of the room were full of shadows and whispers. His eyes moved continuously to each of the danger points: far left corner… stairs… far right corner… stairs… near left corner… stairs… near right corner. Nothing.

Alfie approached the foot of the stairs. His feet began tackling each step silently on the thick fabric, dreading the sound of a creak in the floorboards. He was certain he was being watched. Those darkened corners were full of eyes, watching him ascend the staircase, waiting for him to move deeper into the house.

He reached the top, looked to his left, and then to his right: two windowless hallways, both identical, tunnel-like, with walls matching the colour of the carpet. Blood-red. Remembering the position of the room from his observation point, he turned to his right.

He edged along the corridor sideways, his back brushing the wall, ready to drop to the floor if anyone - or anything - appeared. His imagination was wild. He was sure he could hear the creaking floorboards he narrowly avoided; he was sure he could feel a breath on the back of his neck. But nothing was behind him.

His heart pounded like a banging drum.

A door at the far end of the hallway stood ajar, offering a small chink of light. He continued to edge forward. Muffled voices could be heard, becoming clearer as he approached. This was not in his imagination. Two steps further and he would hear the conversation.

"One more step and it will be the last you ever take…"

Chapter 17

The voice, although threatening, was a whisper. It didn't belong to The Duke or a death walker. Its owner was somebody who wanted to remain hidden.

"Who are you and what is your business here?" said the whispering voice.

"My name is Alfie Andrews, and I have been sent here to investigate this house by a government organisation led by Bruce Spencer … I know who you are."

There was no response. Alfie continued.

"The Organisation will be pleased you are alive and well."

She allowed Alfie to carefully turn and face her. Her striking brown eyes, framed by long eyelashes, were bright in contrast to the dark surroundings. They expressed a mixture of emotions: a fiery determination, hiding a sadness that lay deep within her heart.

Skye placed her index finger to her lips and crept past Alfie, signalling him to follow. They moved closer to the room occupied by The Duke. The muffled conversation was much clearer.

"The transformation of the guards has not developed at the rate I had hoped. They should be more advanced." The voice belonged to The Duke. It was hauntingly calm.

"We have increased the dosage, Master." A second voice was heard, deep and grizzly.

"They will be ready in a few days…" confirmed the calm voice. "And then we can begin."

"How big is the town, Master?"

"Size is of little importance. Its popularity is its downfall. Littered with filthy tourists, spreading their happiness like the plague. The Organisation will fail to cover this one up."

"Your plan, Master, will be executed to perfection."

"Is the other voice the sixth death walker?" whispered Alfie.

Skye's black curls moved up and down, indicating a nod.

"Can you see them?" he asked.

The curls moved from side to side.

Alfie crawled around Skye on his forearms and knees to secure a better position. The door allowed a small gap to see through. Alfie could make out the death walker: bigger and stronger than the others, and much more comfortable with his transformation. He strained his neck further, hoping to lay eyes on The Duke, attempting to see past the death walker's huge frame. He could only hear his chilling voice. "I want to see faces of fear as I look into their eyes and take their life from them … happiness to darkness … just like in Scotland."

Alfie reacted first, managing to place a hand over Skye's mouth before her rage erupted. He used his other arm to attempt to drag her away from the room, but she was surprisingly strong. The struggle alerted the attention of both inside the room. Footsteps pounded their way to the door.

"We've got to get out of here!" hissed Alfie through gritted teeth, now using all his strength to force Skye in the opposite direction. Skye's voice was still trying to force its way through Alfie's clasped hand, but the sight of the death walker, now heavily in pursuit, seemed to encourage her to move in Alfie's direction more freely.

They ran.

Alfie could feel the death walker gaining, moving effortlessly in comparison to the guards. He almost allowed the death walker to close further, daring him to lunge forward. The oversized creature flung himself through the air, his muscular arms outstretched. But he grabbed at nothing as both Skye and Alfie turned sharp left and tumbled down the stairs. Landing together in a heap, they shot to their feet and bolted out of the door.

Alfie had hoped to see the guards still mesmerised by the laser, but all five were positioned on the bridge in a single line, salivating at the sight of the two newcomers.

"I say we go back in and finish that murderer!" yelled Skye uncontrollably, tears streaming down her shiny face.

"Skye, we can't compete with that death walker, let alone Cassian Duke," said Alfie, without taking his eyes off the bridge. "We'll come back and finish this, but not now, not with the light fading - it puts us at an even greater risk."

"Do you promise?" she asked, a vulnerability showing in her eyes.

"I promise," said Alfie, squeezing her hand.

Alfie's mind assessed its options. Running around the outside of the lake would lead them away from the house - eventually. The chances of outrunning the sixth and most advanced death walker, however, was slim. Alfie locked eyes on the bridge once more. He watched the drool hang stubbornly from the chins of the death walkers before falling onto the wooden panels, leaving patches of slobber that glistened in the moonlight.

"Skye, after three, follow me and do exactly what I do," he said.

"I hope you know what you're doing, Alfie Andrews," she responded.

"1 … 2 …"

The door behind them opened, revealing the sixth monstrous death walker, ducking under the door frame to step outside, hungry for revenge.

"THREEEEEEEEEE!"

Alfie grabbed Skye's hand once again and surged forward, charging furiously at the first startled death walker on the bridge. Moments before the impending collision, they dropped to their knees and used the river of drool to slide through the death walkers' legs, avoiding each of their clumsy attempts to reach down and grab at them.

The sixth death walker had frantically rushed

the bridge and crashed into the first guard, creating a domino effect of falling death walkers, one by one. Attempts to scramble to their feet made the situation worse as they fell over each other once again, growling at one another through a pile of tangled limbs.

Alfie and Skye fled, determined to reach the railway track and slip into the darkness. A quick glance behind him saw the death walkers still struggling to their feet. But it was the sight above that caught Alfie's eye. A sight that Alfie knew, right at that moment, would appear in his nightmares for many years to come.

The figure of The Duke of Darkness in the window, waiting with a sinister smile carved into his face, preparing for their return.

Chapter 18

The mission members were greeted by applause on their return to headquarters. It wasn't for Alfie. All eyes and smiles were for Skye. The news of her safe return was a lift for everyone associated with the mission. She represented information that would be crucial in the downfall of The Duke.

An assortment of mouth-watering food covered the table, which had previously been used for the mission meeting. Dozens of pizzas of all varieties were waiting to be devoured in celebration, with sugary and iced doughnuts for dessert. Alfie hadn't eaten all day, and judging by Skye's hungry eyes, she hadn't eaten for a week.

"My son thought pizza would be the perfect choice," said Bruce, sitting at his desk, a glass of whiskey beside him waiting to be sipped. "Personally, I prefer a greasy burger after a fact-finding mission," he added.

Bruce Spencer's eyes rested on Alfie for just a

brief moment, a look of disappointment written across his face, confirming his feelings towards Alfie's spontaneous actions. It was a reaction far worse than any Alfie had expected, even dreaded.

"Well, Skye," said Bruce, looking at the feast, "I think the gentlemanly thing to say is … ladies first."

Skye approached the buffet, quickly followed by Rockwell and McKenzie and a hesitant Alfie.

"Not you, Alfie," spoke Mr Spencer for the first time.

"There's a seat over there for you." Alfie was led away from the feast by his former teacher and sat in a chair in the far corner. "My father has been the head of this organisation since it was founded twenty years ago. Apart from Cassian Duke, you are the first and only member to have ever disobeyed a direct instruction. If I were you, I would stay put and keep it shut."

Damien Spencer re-joined the team and helped himself to a slice of pizza.

For a few minutes, the members ate in silence, watched by Bruce, who remained at his desk, occasionally sipping his drink. Skye had matched Rockwell and McKenzie slice for slice and was now selecting a handful of doughnuts.

"He calls it transformation juice," she said eventually, after she'd eaten her fourth doughnut and another meat-feast slice of pizza.

"What's transformation juice?" asked Bruce calmly.

"The stuff he uses to transform the death walkers—to do what he does. They're unrecognisable from Scotland. I've spent months and months trying to work out who he's taken. They're not my parents—that I do know. Do you know what else I know?" Bruce signalled for her to continue. "That my parents are dead."

The words hung thickly in the air. Alfie remembered Skye's choice of word to describe The Duke outside the house when they were attempting to escape the death walkers: murderer.

"I'm sorry for your loss, Skye," said Bruce, compassion in his voice.

Skye looked vacantly at nothing in particular, processing the information she already knew.

"One of the death walkers is more advanced than the others," she said, shrugging off the negative thoughts. "Goes by the name of Lazarus. He was injected with the juice, whereas the others drank it. The man responsible for the death of my parents was experimenting with the best method to cause further pain and suffering to innocent people."

"How did you find him, Skye?" Bruce asked.

"I hid."

"Impossible. We searched every inch of that town."

"I was hiding where you couldn't search … in the house, the same house he's living in now … just a different place."

There was no response to Skye's statement. Instead, the senior members of The Organisation approached the desk and involved themselves in a serious-looking conversation that was forbidden to the ears of the younger members. Skye looked at Alfie, who was miserably slumped in his chair. She mouthed the words 'what have you done wrong?' before turning back to the members who had positioned themselves behind their leader. He spoke.

"My dear Skye, The Organisation is committed to avenging the death of your parents and preserving the memory of your town. In order for us to achieve this, we need all the information you have. Help us to destroy him, Skye."

Alfie watched as Skye moved purposefully

across the room, pulling out a crumpled piece of paper from her denim pocket and offering it to Bruce Spencer. "Read it…" she said, "to everyone…" offering a quick glance to Alfie.

Bruce Spencer began to read.

To Whom It May Concern,

My name is Skye Nightingale and I am currently pursuing the man responsible for the death of my parents, and the invasion and destruction of my home town in Scotland. His name is Cassian Duke and he is extremely dangerous.

Mr Duke has the ability to transform a person into a walking corpse by looking at them directly in the eye. His eyes light up like fire against the night sky and within seconds their soul seems to become separated from their body.

He takes six of these 'death walkers' and feeds them 'transformation juice', turning them into mighty beasts who have similar powers. He is creating an army.

"Skye, we already know this information," said Bruce matter-of-factly, looking up from the page.

"Turn over," she said.

I need to inform you that the ruthless attack on my town is just the beginning. His next target is a densely populated town in the Lake District. Major cities will eventually be targeted and he won't stop until every chosen human in the United Kingdom becomes a death walker.

Destroying this man will be your biggest challenge. During my time pursuing him, Mr Duke would regularly speak of his immortality as a result of the transformation juice. Residents from my town attempted an attack without success. His skin is impenetrable and he seems impervious to pain.

What I do know is that he must be stopped. If you are reading this—whoever you are—then you have to find the right people to do something, somehow.

Skye

"I lived with the fear I would be caught spying," she explained further. "He would've turned me into a death walker immediately. So I wrote a letter. The world would know the truth and eventually the information would reach you."

"We need to attack with full force!" snarled Rockwell, fuelled by rage and revenge. "Blow up the house with Cassian and the death walkers inside."

"We are a secret government organisation, Rockwell," replied Damien. "Think logically. Questions will be asked after an explosion. What will the PM say?"

"Send the kid in with weapons then," spoke McKenzie. "We'll train him up; he's certainly upped his Courage rating after his refusal to follow orders."

Alfie would've enjoyed the compliment, but a steely stare from Bruce Spencer sent his Courage rating crashing back to earth like a dysfunctional plane.

"HAVE YOU ALL LOST YOUR MINDS?" thundered Bruce unexpectedly. It was the first time Alfie had witnessed him lose his temper in person and his members, particularly McKenzie, were suddenly fixated on their army boots in an attempt to avoid his scathing glare. "The success of this organisation has been built on our ability to plan precise missions that protects our secrecy. Now all of a sudden, YOU want to blow things up and YOU want children to use weapons beyond their capabilities. We need an effective strategy to deal with The Duke without creating a media storm."

"It's the second time I've heard that," spoke Alfie for the first time, thoughts churning inside his head.

"Heard what?" asked Bruce impatiently.

"His eyes light up like fire against the night sky. Mr Spencer said it during our journey back to my holiday home and now Skye has written it … he can only create death walkers in darkness."

"He's right," added Skye. "It only ever

happened at night."

"What are you trying to say, Alfie?" asked Mr Spencer calmly.

"We have to target his main strength," he answered. "We have to target his eyes at their most powerful … the point of alteration … when the human becomes a death walker."

"And how do you suggest we do that?"

Alfie had no idea who asked the question. Like a clearing mist, he could see an idea glowing brightly, like a neon sign. "In your letter, Skye," continued Alfie, "you mentioned the process taking a few seconds. How many seconds?"

"Ten seconds," she responded. "Their shocked or scared expressions become … expressionless."

"Then we have enough time to target the eye." Alfie sprang to his feet and paced the room. "We return to the house at night … we allow him to capture one of us … make him think we are defenceless … wait for his eyes to glow … and we strike … we fire something straight into his eye … something that will cause damage beyond repair… a slingshot or a —"

"I know what we can use," said Bruce.

"This is a huge risk," spoke Mr Spencer,

looking from his father to Alfie. "If anything goes wrong—"

"Alfie will execute the plan to the best of his ability." The words spoken by Bruce Spencer ended any further complaints from his son and confirmed who he had chosen to be sacrificed to The Duke.

"Let me be the one," said Skye defiantly. "I want to see the look on his face."

"No Skye," said Bruce. "You will assist Alfie as you know the house better than anyone, but the rage still burns brightly inside you. Calmness is the best weapon to defeat the chaos."

"Sir, if I may…" Alfie spoke. "I have more thoughts…" Alfie was now positioned next to Skye, and both stood facing the four senior members as if auditioning for a part in a play. The silence encouraged him to continue. "Mr Spencer is right to be concerned. I'm putting my life into the hands of a very dangerous man. If we get that far. The death walkers will be expecting us; they'll be even bigger and stronger as a result of the transformation juice. I want to maximise my chances of success."

"Make your point, young man," urged Bruce.

"We need a third member…"

An outbreak of arguments erupted as all

members immediately knew his intentions.

"We spent nearly a year selecting a suitable candidate and now he wants to bring his friend along!" said Rockwell, with McKenzie nodding in agreement.

"We cannot recruit yet another member," said Mr Spencer.

"Why do you feel we need a third member?" asked Bruce, his question slicing through the disputes.

"The safety of Skye is our greatest concern," answered Alfie. "If I fail, Skye will go on the attack. We need someone to keep her calm, to help her escape from Cassian once more."

"Send Alfie alone," argued McKenzie. "Turn this into an individual mission."

"The last time I sent someone on a full, individual mission was when I sent Cassian into the desert." Bruce gave McKenzie a hard stare before turning his attention back to Alfie.

"And what if the third member's qualities prevent him from seeing the house?"

Alfie was now being interviewed by the boss.

"Then Skye and I will continue alone. Faz will protect the secrecy of The Organisation. I trust him with my life; he's my best friend."

Bruce Spencer dragged his fingers and thumb through his beard harshly, deep in thought. Mr Spencer, along with Rockwell and McKenzie, exchanged anxious looks, waiting for the decision.

"Operation MACER will begin just before dusk tomorrow," announced Bruce Spencer. "Alfie will enter the house with the intention of being captured. Rockwell and McKenzie will continue their role as foot soldiers, and Alfie will be accompanied by Skye and nobody else. We simply cannot recruit a new member the evening before full mission."

Alfie accepted the decision with a respectful nod. Nothing had changed in his mind; he knew that involving Faz was crucial in executing his plan.

It looked like the rules would be broken once more.

Chapter 19

MISSION DAY

Convincing Faz to join the mission was like offering a sweet to a child. Alfie had spent the next morning explaining to his best friend every aspect of how his life had changed so dramatically. He had included everything: the Rockwell and McKenzie observations, Mr Spencer's undercover role as their teacher, Bruce Spencer and the recruitment process of The Organisation, Cassian Duke's destruction of the town and his plans to take over the country, the house that could only be seen by certain children, the fact-finding mission, the death walkers, the rescuing of Skye, and finally Operation MACER.

Hearing himself sharing the events of the past few months made him realise how mind-boggling it must have sounded to somebody who wasn't directly involved in the mission.

Faz's reaction was Faz all over. "This. Sounds.

Awesome!" he said. "It's like James Bond, Indiana Jones and The Bodyguard all rolled into one."

"The Bodyguard?" asked Alfie.

"It's a film about this cool guy who's hired to protect this famous pop singer from some psychopath. She ends up falling in love with him because he's totally awesome and he saves the day. What's this Skye like? Is she pretty?"

Apart from questioning Faz's Modesty rating and considering the chances of the new member actually seeing the house, let alone protecting Skye, Alfie spent the rest of the day continuing the pretence of his imaginary illness. Faz had miraculously caught a more severe version, and both were lying in their beds, moaning and groaning.

"What you need is to be left alone to sleep this off!" prescribed Mrs Andrews, falling headfirst into their trap whilst buttoning her coat in preparation for another day of sightseeing with the miserable-looking Mr Andrews.

"Now, you have to remember that the Spencer's—and Rockwell and McKenzie—have refused to allow you to be part of the mission," explained Alfic, after hearing the front door close.

"But I think I've found a way to get you from here to the house. You're not claustrophobic, are you?"

"Nah, I love spiders," said Faz, "even the big ones that are the size of dinner plates." Faz made a spider with his hand and attacked his own face.

"That's arachnophobic, Faz," corrected Alfie. "I'm talking about claustrophobic: scared of being in a tight space."

"Me? If I ever get trapped in a tight space, I'd just fall asleep."

"Well, you can't do that either: you snore like thunder! Oh, and one other thing… you'll need a backpack."

*

At 7pm, Alfie stood waiting for the arrival of Rockwell and McKenzie. Despite the warnings, he stared up at the golden disc that dominated the sky, chasing away any clouds that threatened. Soon, a blanket of darkness would swallow up the brightness and Alfie would meet his fate.

The sinking feeling in his stomach returned once again.

The BMW trickled to a standstill and two familiar-looking men exited the vehicle. Alfie glanced nervously across the road to where Faz was nestled behind a line of trees, a look of horror carved into his face. Alfie had forgotten what an intimidating sight the two men were.

"Can you open the boot?" Alfie asked. "I need to put my bag inside."

"Why have you brought a bag?" asked a suspicious-looking Rockwell.

"Water. What with the heat and this mission, I've been getting headaches." Alfie rubbed his forehead and grimaced. "Also, Bruce mentioned a weapon… I wasn't sure of the size."

Both Rockwell and McKenzie pondered his comments for a few seconds, before Rockwell took his bag and McKenzie opened the boot.

"What's this scratch on the side of your car?" offered Alfie theatrically.

Panicked, Rockwell and McKenzie bolted around to the driver's side where Alfie was crouching, leaving the opened boot unattended.

"Where?"

"There!"

"WHERE??"

"THERE!!"

As Rockwell and McKenzie attempted to locate the imaginary scratch on the side of their beloved car, they didn't see the figure appear from the side of the road and slide into the boot.

"Sorry!" Alfie said, "I'm sure I saw a scratch. The brightness of the sun and these headaches are playing tricks on my eyes."

Alfie opened the driver side door for Rockwell, before scurrying to the rear of the car to check Faz (who was curled up beneath a blanket with one thumb pointing upwards). He closed the boot quickly.

"Let's get going!" he chirped enthusiastically. "We don't want to keep Bruce waiting."

*

An identical vehicle was waiting on the edge of the woodland as the car pulled up an hour later. Doors opened simultaneously as four senior members and two junior members stepped out and faced each other. Alfie had been instructed to wear his black combat trousers and army boots, along with a black T-shirt. Skye was dressed identically. Her black curls were tied back to prevent them from invading her face, further revealing her olive-skinned complexion. So too, dressed in black, were Rockwell and McKenzie, dwarfing the younger members. With Bruce and Damien Spencer wearing immaculate black suits, and the addition of the black BMWs glistening in the evening sun, an onlooker would have witnessed a scene from an action movie that Faz would've adored.

Faz? How would he escape the boot?

"How are the pre-mission nerves, young Alfie?" asked Bruce, his blue tie and matching handkerchief adding a splash of colour to his dark suit.

"I'm fine… thanks," Alfie responded. "Just a little headache."

"The weapon is known as the arctic spyder," explained Bruce, showing little empathy, considering it was a MACER characteristic. He removed the torch-like device from his pocket. "It is the world's most powerful handheld laser; 8,000 times brighter than looking directly at the sun."

Bruce Spencer pointed the laser at Rockwell and McKenzie's car. A thin, blindingly pink beam exploded from the device and within seconds, a swirl of dancing blue smoke appeared.

"Boss, the car!" pleaded Rockwell.

Bruce chuckled, shutting off the device a few moments later to add to their misery. He turned to Alfie. "This laser can be seen from space; it can start a fire; it can even cook popcorn. Just imagine the damage it can cause to the eyes of Cassian Duke."

Alfie took the laser from his boss and tested the weight by moving his hand up and down. "Excellent choice, Sir."

"Okay then," spoke Damien, his splash of colour a bright yellow, "we have the weapon, we have Alfie and Skye, and we have about thirty minutes before nightfall. Skye has been briefed and will be communicating with us at all times. So you, Alfie, can concentrate on the mission."

"Any questions?" said Bruce.

"Can I get my bag from the boot of the car?" Alfie asked.

Bruce's eyes narrowed with suspicion. "What bag?"

"He's brought along a bag," answered McKenzie, "contains water to keep him hydrated."

Bruce stared at Alfie, his eyes burning holes into his lies more powerfully than Cassian and the laser put together. "Go with him, McKenzie," he spoke, turning and heading back to his car…" Oh, and McKenzie… check the bag."

Alfie contemplated the consequences of McKenzie finding Faz hidden in the boot of the car. The best possible scenario would be his immediate removal from the mission. The worst scenario wasn't worth considering. How far were The Organisation willing to go to protect their secrecy?

As McKenzie unlocked the boot, Alfie squeezed his eyes tightly shut. It was a technique he often used as a younger boy when something scared him late at night. It was as if he was able to shut himself inside his body to warn off negative thoughts.

He opened them slowly. The boot was empty.

Relief washed over him, dissolving the tension that had started to suffocate his lungs. He looked to his right and watched McKenzie unzip a familiar-looking bag…

Faz had escaped successfully and left a bottle of water in his backpack.

Chapter 20

Alfie and Skye disappeared into the dense woodland and soon a fiery water colour of pink, orange and yellow invaded the sky. They followed a path that naturally led to the railway track, occasionally stepping over and pulling aside overgrown branches that stood in their way. Conversation was limited between the two as the enormity of the task descended upon them. This time, Alfie knew he would come face to face with Cassian and his lack of preparation swamped his mind.

His last-minute planning was interrupted by Skye. The sound of her footsteps had silenced, and Alfie turned to see her pulling out something from her pocket. A notepad and pen appeared, and she approached Alfie, scribbling something on the paper. The last rays of sun were fading, but there was enough light for Alfie to read the words written:

Where are we meeting, Faz?

The question was a representation of Skye's

intelligence. Not only had she predicted his plans, but she was keeping it hidden from Bruce and Damien. Alfie was immediately impressed. He took the pen and scribbled his response:

By the railway track. How did you know?

She smiled, enjoying the fact that her prediction was correct, and took the notepad and pen once more. Skye wrote her response whilst talking into the microphone. "We're just drawing a map to remind ourselves of the route," she told her superiors. She handed Alfie the notepad with a wink.

Only known you for 24hrs and you haven't once followed an order!! Bruce and Damien will freak when they see Faz. Leave it to me…

They continued in silence. Dusk began to settle like a warm blanket covering the land. The deeper they went, the darker it became. The reduced amount of light pollution allowed the stars to glisten like expensive diamonds.

Finally, they reached the railway track. A wide-framed silhouette could be seen as they approached, clicking a torch on and off as a signal. The voice confirmed who it was. "Well, about time…" bellowed Faz through the encroaching darkness, "I nearly gave up and went home."

"Faz, meet Skye," said Alfie.

"The pleasure is all mine, madam," said Faz, with a theatrical bow.

"Does he always talk this loud?" she responded, which made Faz straighten up stiffly.

"Pass me my bag, Alfie," Faz said, rather obviously reducing the volume, which made Skye smirk. "I'm parched."

Faz unzipped the bag, pushed the water bottle to one side, pulled out and discarded what looked like a magazine with the title 'Woodland Survival', and reached for an energy drink, which he opened and swigged until the can was empty. Both Alfie and Skye stared at him.

"What? A tired man is full of mistakes," he said.

"And a boy full of sugar is a boy with heart disease!" added Skye.

Skye held her hand in the air to prevent Faz from responding; the other was pressed to her ear. News had travelled quickly.

"Yes Sir, I can confirm it is Faz…"

Alfie could picture the look of horror on the faces of both Bruce and Damien. To them, the thought of being disobeyed a second time was unthinkable. Skye continued.

"He has informed us that he travelled in the boot of Rockwell and McKenzie's car after becoming suspicious of Alfie's unusual behaviour…"

Suspicious? An overly curious friend taking matters into his own hands, desperate to find out the truth? Skye was doing an excellent job.

"Sir, if this information gets back to the PM, it will not reflect well on The Organisation…"

Clever move. Alfie knew one thing for certain: Bruce Spencer placed the reputation of The Organisation above anything else.

"This can only be resolved by pretending that we had recruited him as a member and allowing him to be part of the mission…"

Alfie and Faz waited in anticipation for the response, with Skye listening intently to the message she was receiving.

"Thank you, Sir and yes, I can confirm that Faz is to be trusted … and no, Alfie was completely unaware."

Skye grabbed the torch from Faz and positioned it between her teeth, the light shining on her notepad. Alfie and Faz positioned themselves on either side of Skye and read her message:

Even the most powerful of men are easy to control. Now, let's pay a visit to a house.

Chapter 21

The house could be seen in the distance as the trio began their slow walk through the passageway. Alfie was sure he could see eyes watching them through the trees, their trunks framed against the moon like bars of a prison.

Soon he would be the prisoner.

The pace of their footsteps had dropped considerably, none of the members wanting to face the consequences of reaching the end of the passage. The deathly silence was broken only occasionally by Skye talking quietly into her microphone, updating her superiors on their progress.

The house was beginning to draw near.

"Alfie?" asked a trembling voice through the darkness. "What's the plan when we reach the house?"

He couldn't answer his best friend's question. Apart from the previous evening's overtired idea of targeting the eye, Alfie hadn't considered how he would slip past the death walkers a second time, let alone getting close to The Duke.

He had never felt so unprepared.

The passageway came to an end and the mission members positioned themselves in the shadows of the trees to gather their thoughts and observe the scene.

"The death walkers look stronger, more advanced."

Alfie wasn't sure who Skye was talking to but she was correct in her observation. All five of the death walkers no longer looked trapped in their own body, waiting for their brain to catch up. Instead, they were moving freely and drinking thirstily from a transparent bottle holding fluorescent pink liquid.

"Transformation juice," she added.

The door was being guarded by Lazarus, a flickering light above him occasionally illuminating his murderous face. Alfie was able to study Lazarus more closely from a safer distance. Both his ears and nostrils were pierced with golden hoops, adding to his terrifying appearance. His hair was long and matted and slicked back into a ponytail whereas the other death walkers were bald. The creature was holding a syringe filled with the glowing liquid as an alternative to the bottled form. He extended his muscular arm and jabbed the needle recklessly into his skin. The three stunned observers could visibly see the pink fluid coursing through his veins, injecting supernatural life into his already phenomenal size.

Eventually, Alfie broke the silence. "Faz? Can you see what we see?"

Alfie could only rely on the voice of his best friend as the darkness filled his space. But no reply came.

"Faz?"

There were few things that left Faz speechless. He had clearly passed the MACER test and his reward was the sight of six creatures that had terrified him into silence.

"There are so many things that could go wrong," explained Skye, too impatient to wait for a response from Faz. "If you surrender yourself to the death walkers, chances are they will either rip you into little pieces or turn you into one of them."

Operation MACER had taught Alfie quite quickly that Skye didn't have a problem sharing her thoughts and getting straight to the point.

"We need you alive for The Duke," she added

bluntly.

Alfie and Skye left Faz to his own thoughts and watched as the death walkers continued their patrol.

"How about swimming in the lake?" suggested Skye.

Alfie had already considered and dismissed the idea. "I can't risk the laser in the water."

"Okay," Skye pressed, "so we use the laser to distract them."

"That's how I snuck past them yesterday," he answered. "And anyway, the arctic spyder is our secret weapon for The Duke."

Alfie searched for a solution, but his brain was a maze of dead ends. Skye's suggestions had faded like the sun. And where was the tactical plan from The Organisation with years of mission experience?

"They all take a drink at exactly the same time." It was the first time Faz had spoken in the twenty minutes they had been watching the house. "I've watched them do it twice," he continued, "they guzzle their drink for around fifteen seconds whilst looking at the moon. I counted."

Alfie knew the reason why his best friend was sharing this information. "Fifteen seconds, you say?" he asked.

"No more, no less," answered Faz.

"Then it will give me enough time to make it to the house without them noticing."

"You seem to be forgetting about Lazarus," interjected Skye.

"Lazarus injects the fluid at the same time," explained Faz. "He watches the fluid travel through his system, almost admires it. He is completely captivated by the process. He's unaware of anything else."

Alfie smiled. Not only had Faz's observations silenced his biggest critic, but it had confirmed that it had been the right decision to recruit him. Nobody could analyse a situation to the finest of detail quite like Faz.

Alfie readjusted his position and now looked like a sprinter at the start line.

"As soon as they take their drink, I'm making a run for it. Faz, I just hope you've got this right…"

Three pairs of eyes were fixated on the bottles clasped in the hands of the death walkers, the liquid lighting up like neon signs against the darkness.

Slowly, as one, arms began to lift and heads began to tilt as the bottles moved in the direction of their salivating mouths.

"GO!" ordered Faz.

Alfie bolted forward as fast as his legs could carry him, past the first death walker, then the second, then the third, between the fourth and fifth, and then onto the bridge. He stayed light on his feet as he rushed towards Lazarus, whose bulbous eyes were preoccupied by the hypnotic liquid snaking through his veins. Alfie skidded to a halt, somehow managing to avoid the oversized limbs of the injection-fuelled death walker, and slipped into the house unnoticed.

Alfie closed the heavy door and rested his head against it. His lungs were screaming for more oxygen, and he desperately sucked in the heavy air around him.

He knew almost immediately. He didn't need to see him. He could feel his presence like an unwanted illness.

"I had a strange feeling…" came a voice that was piercingly deep, creating an echo that vibrated through the air, "…that the darkness would invite a very special guest this evening.

Chapter 22

The voice sent fear racing through Alfie's system. It flooded his muscles, paralysing his movement; it swamped his mind, suffocating his thought capacity; it invaded his heart and reached deep into his soul.

"You've been here before," came the voice again, accusingly. "A new member of The Organisation, no doubt."

Alfie remained rooted to the same spot, still facing the door he had entered. With his back to The Duke and the laser in his pocket, he was in the best possible position in the worst possible situation.

"I'm in the wrong place," responded Alfie, almost apologetically.

"The evidence suggests otherwise," came the voice once more. "Escaping Lazarus proves you're athletic, taking on my guards shows courage, and only a resilient fool returns for more. You showed empathy towards that pathetic girl and your modesty stops you from realising the talents you have."

Pathetic? The girl escaped and survived for months after witnessing the death of her parents. Anger rose inside Alfie, dissolving the fear like an effective dose of medicine. But he needed to remain calm. Bruce Spencer's words circulated his mind: Calmness is the best weapon to defeat the chaos.

"I was lost in the darkness," spoke Alfie.

"NEVER blame the darkness," roared The Duke, slicing through Alfie's anger. Cassian's tone softened and began to purr. "The darkness offers opportunity; it is where the greatest work can be done. The darkness opens your mind and allows you to realise the truth. Do you want to know what the truth is, Alfie Andrews?"

It was clear that Cassian knew more than The Organisation had expected. But how? Alfie pushed the thought aside. He needed to concentrate on playing the game to the rules of The Duke.

"I would like to know," said Alfie.

"Then look me in the eye and show the respect I deserve."

It was a huge risk but a calculated one: Alfie sensed that The Duke was enjoying having a new audience and wanted it to continue.

He turned slowly and lifted his eyes cautiously…

The candlesticks did not offer enough light to fully reveal the man stood at the top of the staircase, the darkness desperate to keep hold of its master. The silhouette began to descend the stairs.

"The truth, Alfie Andrews…" it spoke, "is that despite sitting at the top of the food chain, humans are the most pathetic species walking the planet. They have all the power but no purpose. They simply exist. Their ambitions are overshadowed by their emotions: love, happiness, fear, sadness." Venom and hatred dripped from every word he spoke. "It clouds their vision and infects their minds. Only a select few have ever risen up and achieved real greatness."

"I want to share a story, Alfie … a story of where I found my true purpose."

Each step took The Duke closer to the light that covered the lower half of the staircase. He continued.

"In my former life, a particular mission left me at the point of no return. Exhausted, I was lost in the unforgiving desert, battling temperatures beyond my human capability. No food, no water, no communication. Death was so close it was like a reflection in the mirror."

He moved ever closer to the light.

"At my most desperate, I saw this... this glow... in the near distance. It was the most beautiful image I had ever seen..."

"... As I approached, I felt this magnetic force, this emotion, this supreme strength growing inside me, pulling me closer to this luminous light hidden in the sand..."

Almost his entire body was revealed by the light. A full-length black coat surrounded his army boots and trousers.

"...I buried my hands deep into the sand, searching for the glow that radiated beneath the surface. My fingers made contact with an object, which I immediately removed. The object was a transparent canister holding a thick, syrupy liquid. Attached was a beautiful pendant filled with the same fluid..."

Alfie could see the pendant hanging from a chain around the throbbing neck of The Duke, the green liquid glistening in the darkness.

"I drank the sweet nectar. It slipped down my throat and ignited life into my tired muscles. It made me feel invincible. But that wasn't the best part…"

Cassian Duke's face finally entered the pool of light, his mouth twisting into a savage sneer which revealed a row of black teeth. His face seemed eyeless, only thick, black shadows surrounded his sockets. But then the eyes appeared. A dull yellow with black predatorial slits for pupils, before disappearing once again into the shadows.

"Thoughts poured into my mind," he continued, his eyes continuing to appear and disappear, "so clear that they swept away any emotions that overpower the ordinary brain. These thoughts announced my destiny: to conquer and rule. The thoughts told me to seek out the strong and destroy the weak; to create a new species of superiority to follow me on my journey."

His voice deepened further into a growl. "I will wipe out anyone and everyone: royal families, powerful governments, even the most advanced militaries… And I will transform the lucky ones."

"Would you like to be a chosen one, Alfie Andrews?"

Alfie was unable to consider the question. He was trembling uncontrollably and sweat droplets were snaking down the side of his face. He needed to think clearly, but the sight of the man before him reduced Alfie to a pile of rubble.

He collected his thoughts. You have the laser, maintain his trust.

"I am honoured to be considered, Sir," responded Alfie with a respectful nod.

The Duke's twisted smile widened further, revealing overly defined wrinkles set deep into his face. He took a long, deep breath, inhaling the power and control he had over his guest.

"I often wondered who would be the first after Scotland," he finally spoke, following a long silence that lingered in the air.

He continued his journey to the foot of the stairs.

"I considered the girl for a while, but I began to enjoy her misery, along with her pathetic attempts to conceal her presence in the house."

Black leather gloves were being removed from his pocket.

"Of course, it had to be a child … children are easily controlled."

The gloves were now being carefully placed on each hand; every finger being squeezed methodically into place.

"And that child had to be gifted. After all, the

curse I placed on the house was very specific."

The Duke watched his own fingers as they extended outwards, back and forth, to stretch the leather of the glove into the correct position.

"She was gifted, Alfie Andrews, but I wanted someone who had been selected ... someone who had been recruited ..."

He reached the bottom of the stairs. His wild eyes now seemed to be ever-present, toxic with an evil ambition.

"Someone just like you."

Chapter 23

Alfie felt his trouser pocket for the comfort of the laser. It was his only hope of survival. Every muscle demanded him to turn and run, to escape the nightmare that had spilled over to reality. He craved his old life: sitting at home listening to his mother lecture his father about the importance of a work-life balance. Instead, he faced a man so contaminated by evil that he belonged in the deepest, darkest region of hell.

Slowly, The Duke lifted the sizable collar on his full-length coat. First the gloves, now the collar.

He was preparing for the transformation.

"These are your final moments of life as you know it," he spoke, his voice vibrating venomously around the hallway. "Are you ready to be reborn?"

Alfie struggled to control the fear climbing his throat. Adrenaline charged around his body like a racing car and his blonde hair was plastered against his scalp with sweat. He reached into his pocket and attempted to collect the laser in his hand, but his fingers were moist and clumsy. Panic rose in his chest like floodwater.

Remain calm, he told himself.

The Duke's ritual continued. He removed the chain from around his neck and rested the glowing pendant in his fingers. He gazed at its beauty as if it were his newborn child—his cold eyes momentarily overcome by affection. But then the twisted smile returned once more, and his nostrils began to flare with anticipation.

Alfie watched on. The Duke unscrewed the top and lifted the tubular pendant towards his blistered lips as if to take a drink. Instead, to Alfie's disbelief, the liquid was poured directly into each of his eyes, causing a pulsating glow that moved quickly from pink to yellow.

The glow blinded Alfie, and by the time his own eyes had adjusted, he had already lost valuable seconds.

The sight was more terrifying than before. The Duke was stood, arms outstretched sideways, muttering ritual chants about the darkness, his eyes continually rolling into the back of his head.

The transformation process had begun.

Instinctively, Alfie attempted to break eye contact and take a step backwards. This proved impossible. His eyes became uncontrollably locked in the direction of The Duke and his feet were clamped to the same spot on the carpet. Any further attempts to move his head or feet were unsuccessful. His heart was now battering his ribs and his lungs were screaming with panic.

The laser.

Alfie's fingers had lost contact with the weapon in his pocket. He retrieved it in his hands and used his thumb to search for the activation button.

"The darkness desires you," chanted The Duke, "the darkness demands you to join her…"

Still, Alfie couldn't locate the button. His thumb seemed to lack the coordination required for the simple task.

"Allow the darkness to take control…"

Alfie could feel his heart rate beginning to slow. The urgency of using the laser in the limited amount of time he had drifted nonchalantly to the back of his mind.

He felt a heaviness to his eyelids and a wave of exhaustion spread across him. He fought the tiredness with the determination of a child attempting to stay awake to watch their favourite television programme. But the tiredness was terminal.

The sharpness of his vision was blurring, and the words spoken by Cassian muffling. He was losing the battle.

The… laser…

His brain half-heartedly attempted to connect with his fingers once more. He lifted the now heavy device from his pocket weakly and extended his arm in the direction of the stairs. He watched as the laser slipped from his fingers' grasp and landed on the wooden floor with a clatter, rolling to the feet of The Duke. Alfie's heart didn't react; any hope of surviving the transformation was gone.

The darkness began its approach. It seeped into Alfie's system, through his ears, nose, through the pores in his skin. It trickled into his bloodstream and began to spin its web of blackness.

Spots began to appear in Alfie's vision, growing larger.

Any second now…

Colourful images swam into focus and then accelerated away as the blackness wrapped itself around his eyes like a warm coat.

Any… second… now…

An eruption of noise shook the room as two figures surged through the front door, the heavier one charging at Alfie. The impact lifted his limp body off his feet and he landed heavily on the floor; the momentum skidding him along the smooth surface, away from the magnetic pull of The Duke. The black spots clouding Alfie's vision scattered slightly, allowing him to watch the new series of events unfold.

"I like my best friend just the way he is!" roared Faz, protecting Alfie like a human shield.

"Now!" ordered Skye, who remained pressed against the door, preventing any unwanted visitors from entering.

Faz drew his right arm back behind his head like a baseball pitcher and launched his arm forward. A gold coin was released from his hand. The coin somersaulted repeatedly through the air, glistening magnificently against the darkness. It thundered forward in the direction of The Duke's widening luminous eyes.

All three mission members held their breath. It needed to hit the eye. The room stood still as the coin completed its final rotation, almost in slow motion, and crashed into the right eye of The Duke of Darkness.

The impact forced The Duke's head backwards and a spatter of green blood-like liquid landed on one of the candlesticks at the foot of the stairs. Robotically, he repositioned his head and glared individually at each of the mission members. They stared back, swamped with negativity, and watched.

The Duke stumbled slightly. Green liquid began to trickle from his mouth. He tried to speak; his black teeth coated with the syrup as more poured out. His nose began to leak with the same bright fluid. His other eye, too. Within seconds, the liquid was flowing from every opening, covering his face and dripping onto the floor. The Duke attempted to walk forward in desperation, his glare now fixed solely on Alfie. Still, he staggered forward, swaying from left to right.

And then he stopped and collapsed on the floor.

Chapter 24

1 DAY AFTER MISSION

Alfie's eyes opened. He blinked a few times to allow his vision to swim into focus. A familiar-looking chandelier greeted him, along with furniture that confirmed his whereabouts. He was back at headquarters. An attempt was made to sit upright on a sofa he didn't recognise, but exhaustion prevented this from happening. Instead, he lay in the same position, his brain searching for answers. Mr Spencer appeared in his vision. "Nice to have you back," he said with a smile.

"What happened? Where is everyone?" Alfie asked groggily, accepting a bottle of water from his former teacher.

"You blacked out," he replied. "Your body was overwhelmed by the strength of the transformation attempt."

"Attempt?"

"The mission was a success," came another voice belonging to the leader of The Organisation. Bruce Spencer entered through the same door as before and approached Alfie, who had now managed to drag his tired body into a sitting position and was sipping from his bottle of water. Bruce stood beside him. "You were right all along," he said. "Right to enter the house when instructed not to; right to escape with Skye at sunset to avoid the transformation threat; and most importantly, you were right to recruit a third mission member."

Alfie struggled to accept the compliment. "Sir, I failed," he said with honesty.

Bruce chuckled playfully. The intensity in his eyes from before had washed away. "Your Modesty rating is now officially off the scale." Damien Spencer nodded in agreement, a brilliant smile lighting up his face. "Alfie," Damien spoke, "the mission objective was to wipe out Cassian Duke. You rescued Skye, you suggested we target the eye. You recruited Faz, knowing his ability to throw with accuracy, knowing his coin could be used as a weapon if the laser failed."

Mr Spencer was right. Alfie knew he needed Faz on the mission. Despite his best friend's imperfections, he was brilliantly intelligent, fiercely loyal, and armed with the most lethally accurate right arm at Pleasant Grove.

"Where are they?" he asked.

"They are resting," answered Bruce. "Both refused to leave your side until about an hour ago, when exhaustion finally took over. You've been out for fifteen hours."

Alfie was relieved to hear his friends were alive and well. He looked forward to hearing Faz's version of events. His parents would be worried also to find both beds unoccupied at their holiday accommodation. Alfie hoped his mother would assume a full recovery had been made, and they were exploring what the Lake District had to offer.

"The Duke shared a story…" explained Alfie, refocusing his attention. "He spoke of finding a canister filled with bright liquid—when he was lost in the desert. It was the liquid that gave him his powers." Bruce and Damien Spencer remained silent. They knew there was more Alfie needed to share. "I saw something…" he continued, "when he was transforming me… there are more of these canisters. I saw seven of them. Each canister a different colour, buried in different locations around the world."

"Do you know of these locations, Alfie?" Damien asked.

"No. Nor do I know where they have come from... I just know they exist, waiting to be claimed."

There was silence. Both men were absorbing the information. Alfie looked at Bruce Spencer; his intense stare had returned. "Then there is more work to be done," came his only response.

The tension that surrounded the unwelcoming information was interrupted by a loud entrance from Faz and Skye, followed by Rockwell and McKenzie.

"Alfie!" beamed Faz. "Welcome back to the land of the living!"

"We were so worried, Alfie!" said Skye, rushing over to him and taking his hand. Alfie reddened slightly. Words began to spill out of Faz's mouth. Faz enjoyed sharing stories more than most people, but an overexcited, overtired Faz meant the words gushed out rather than trickled. An endless list of information. "You were ages in that house, Alfie—absolutely ages. You needed us. I said it to Skye. She agreed. I knew you were in trouble—you and I have got this mind connection thing going on.

So Skye lit a fire in the woods. To distract the death walkers. They fell into our trap. We stormed the bridge."

The mission members chuckled at how animated Faz was becoming, reliving the mission like he was a Hollywood star.

"You were not a pretty sight when we entered. Pale face, shivering and sweating at the same time— I didn't even know you could do that. You just seemed locked in your own body. I saw the laser on the floor by The Duke's foot. Plan A aborted! I knew what I had to do. I took the coin from my pocket. Looked directly into the eye of my target and launched the coin through the air. It smashed into his face. Pink liquid everywhere. The Duke was stumbling around. Direct hit! Direct hit! Man down!"

"We carried you out of the house," continued Skye, her words calmer and easier to understand. "The death walkers were lying on the floor also— completely lifeless. By the time we were halfway down the passageway… the house was gone."

"How do we know for sure that he has gone?" Alfie asked.

"Nobody knows anything for sure," said Bruce. "We will monitor… and we will hope."

Alfie's gaze scanned each mission member before resting on Skye. The sadness in her eyes remained. For everyone else, the mission was a triumph. But for Skye, the mission represented the loss of her beloved parents. A terrible tragedy she witnessed with her own eyes. Her mission to avenge the death of her closest family members began that day and lasted for months, living in fear. A mixture of feelings pinballed from his stomach to his heart. There was one emotion, however, that stood out from the rest: empathy. How would she ever recover? And what would happen to this brave and beautiful girl?

"Our time here has ended," announced Bruce, releasing Alfie from his thoughts. He stood and walked over to where Rockwell and McKenzie were standing. "I now must brief the Prime Minister. Congratulations on a successful mission. Great achievements are often based on instinct. The three of you have offered further proof of this. I will leave you in the capable hands of my son, Damien." He continued his walk to the door and disappeared from view.

"Catch you later," said Rockwell with a salute.

"Nice work, fellas," added McKenzie with a

smile. Both followed their boss through the door.

*

Alfie, Faz and Skye nestled into the back of the spacious BMW, eager to remain together. Mr Spencer sat in the driver's seat, started the engine, and eased the car onto the road. The journey back to their holiday accommodation would hopefully answer some lingering questions. An awkward silence filled the interior of the car: nobody really sure of how to approach the subject. Alfie finally spoke. "So… what happens now?"

"You enjoy the rest of your holiday," answered Mr Spencer.

"And Skye?"

"Skye will remain with The Organisation until September," he answered.

"September?" Alfie probed, hopeful.

Mr Spencer smiled. "In September, I will be contacting the head teacher at Pleasant Grove to see if there are any places available for an enthusiastic and intelligent new student."

The shocked and excited expressions from all three of them suggested even Skye was unaware of the decision that had been made. All Alfie knew was that he was the happiest he had ever been. He needed to know more. "Are we still members of The Organisation?" he asked.

"Are you willing to maintain the secrecy of The Organisation?" questioned Mr Spencer. All three backseat passengers nodded eagerly. "Like every mission member," he continued, "if my father believes your skill base is suited to a particular assignment, then you will be contacted…Until then, your number one priority is your education."

Alfie thought back to life at Pleasant Grove. Despite having to suffer Connor DeAngelo—and his ego—on a daily basis, it had been a good year at school. Skye would make it even better. But it had been a good year because Alfie had finally found a teacher who understood and inspired him. Mr Spencer.

"Unfortunately, I won't be joining you in September," said Mr Spencer, reading Alfie's mind once more. "My objective at Pleasant Grove has been achieved." He looked at Alfie through the rear-view mirror and smiled warmly at him.

Alfie and Faz said their goodbyes to Skye and Mr Spencer when the car pulled up outside the holiday accommodation. They promised to meet Skye in September before school started—Bruce

Spencer had contacted her Aunt Agnes, who luckily lived close to their school, and arranged for Skye to stay with her. A promise was also made to Mr Spencer, updating him immediately on Connor's 'ego outbursts' and any future cross-country events. Alfie and Faz roared with laughter when Mr Spencer announced that Mrs Fulford was a better MACER candidate than Connor.

After a final goodbye wave, the boys made their way up the path. "Faz," Alfie said, "I didn't get a chance to say—"

"You would've done the same for me," said Faz, before Alfie could finish his sentence. "It's what best friends do."

They both smiled, before hugging and highfiving and whooping, "We did it!"

"I tell you what," Alfie said, approaching the front door, "that is one awesome coin; don't ever sell it!"

"I was tempted the other day," admitted Faz.

"Why?"

"I found out one was sold at auction for 7.6million. Apparently, it's a legend among collectors."

A thunderous voice coming from inside the house drowned out any reaction to the staggering amount declared by Faz. It belonged to Arthur Andrews.

"The blinkin' Wi-Fi's gone, AGAIN!

ABOUT THE AUTHOR

Oliver Wood was born in Birmingham, England, and spent his childhood exploring a den at the bottom of his garden - creating imaginary world after imaginary world.

One day, whilst teaching a group of rowdy Year 6 children at a local primary school, he came up with an idea for a series of children's adventure books, called The Mission Series. He really hopes you like the first one.

Oliver lives in Henley, in Arden with his wife and three children—the twin boy and girl are proving to be a challenge.

Printed in Great Britain
by Amazon

21006847R00109